Apache Spring

A band of young Apache braves rampages across Dawson County, New Mexico and, when a stagecoach bound for El Paso is held up, all but one of the coach's passengers are massacred. Young Lizzie Reardon, a schoolmistress about to start her first job in Burro Creek is the sole survivor, but she has seen the attacker's faces and is now their target.

Deputy Sheriff Frank McCoy joins forces with famous Kentuckian gunfighter, Jack Stone, to foil the plot. Bullets fly and not all will live to see another day.

Apache Spring

J.D. Kincaid

A Black Horse Western

ROBERT HALE · LONDON

© J.D. Kincaid 2014
First published in Great Britain 2014

ISBN 978-0-7198-1358-0

Robert Hale Limited
Clerkenwell House
Clerkenwell Green
London EC1R 0HT

www.halebooks.com

Typeset by
Derek Doyle & Associates, Shaw Heath
Printed and bound in Great Britain by
CPI Antony Rowe, Chippenham and Eastbourne

ONE

Jack Stone rode his bay gelding nice and easy along the Butterfield stage route on that warm, sun-kissed April afternoon. The Kentuckian was on his way south into Texas and ultimately to San Antonio, where he intended signing up for the cattle drive that each year followed the Western Trail from Texas to Nebraska.

Six foot two inches in his stockinged feet, Stone consisted of nigh on 200 pounds of muscle and bone. Though slow to anger, he displayed when riled a ferocity which had earned him the reputation of being half mountain lion and half grizzly. The years had taken their toll, leaving scars, both mental and physical. The bullet holes had healed, but the broken nose remained and the emotional scars, which made Stone what he was, would never completely heal. His square-cut, deeply lined face had been handsome once and now and again, when he smiled, it regained something of its former good looks.

It was said that Stone was a man born under a wandering star, yet this was not strictly true. It was through circumstance rather than inclination that Jack Stone had become a rover. Born the son of a Kentucky farmer, he most likely would still be farming the family homesteading had not his father been forced to sell it to pay off his gambling debts. Shortly afterwards, his father had been killed in a saloon brawl, and thereafter the widow had struggled, alone and unaided, to bring up her young son. Stone was fourteen years old when, worn out by her efforts, she, too, had died. From that time onwards, he had been on his own.

Stone had tried his hand at most things in his time: farm work, ranch work, riding herd on several cattle drives, some bronco-busting, even a spell working the Colorado gold mines. Then, with the advent of the Civil War, he had fought for the Union and afterwards, for a while, served as an army scout. But the white man's savagery towards his red brother had sickened Stone and he had resigned.

Later, he had worked as a ranch hand in Nevada and met and married Mary Spencer, a local store-keeper's daughter. Once more he had intended to sink roots. But it was not to be, for within a year Mary died in childbirth, with the child still-born. This tragic event had a devastating effect upon him and it was several months before he recovered. He was by then a changed man: a man who would always be moving on, always looking for another frontier to cross.

His reputation as a gunfighter had been earned subsequently, with a series of jobs as a stagecoach guard, deputy US marshal, deputy sheriff and, most famously, sheriff of Mallory, the roughest, toughest town in the state of Colorado. Indeed, it was as the man who tamed Mallory that he had become a legend of the West.

Nowadays Jack Stone was keen to avoid trouble and was looking for a quiet life. But he had to eat. Hence his ride south to San Antonio and his intention to participate in a cattle drive scheduled to commence later in the month.

A tall, broad-shouldered figure attired in a grey Stetson, grey shirt, knee-length buckskin jacket, faded denim pants and unspurred boots, Stone wore a red kerchief round his strong, thick neck and on his right thigh he carried a Frontier Model Colt tied down, while in his saddleboot there rested a Winchester. Both the revolver and the rifle had served the Kentuckian well across the years.

For the present Stone was in no particular hurry. He had plenty of time to reach his destination prior to the commencement of the cattle drive. Consequently, he cantered along at a fairly moderate pace and aimed to rest up for the night at Mesilla, the next town on the trail. He reckoned that sometime the following day he should cross the state line out of New Mexico and into Texas. Then it would be a nice, easy ride south-eastwards through the Lone Star State to San Antonio.

It was when he was two miles short of Mesilla that Stone first became aware of the rider jogging along the trail behind him. How long he had been there Stone could not be sure. The trail had recently begun following the Rio Grande through the foothills of the San Andres mountains, with many a twist and turn. Therefore the horseman was constantly vanishing and then reappearing. The question Stone asked himself was whether the man was actively pursuing him or merely travelling in the same direction?

In an attempt to determine which was the case, Stone reduced the bay gelding's canter to a slow trot. Then he continued for a further quarter of a mile before executing a quick, surreptitious glance over his shoulder. The distance between the Kentuckian and his pursuer remained exactly the same as it had been prior to his slackening the pace. Ergo, the horseman had evidently adjusted his pace to match Stone's.

To be absolutely sure that this was so Stone urged the gelding to resume its normal canter. Another quarter-mile and another backward glance satisfied him that he was indeed being actively pursued, for the distance between himself and the other rider had still not changed.

By now Stone was a little over a mile from Mesilla

and, rather than force a confrontation, he determined to carry on along the trail and into the small township. Once there, he proposed to enter the nearest saloon, slake his thirst and await events.

Stone's changes of pace had given his pursuer pause for thought. He had hoped to take the Kentuckian by surprise, but now was pretty sure he had been rumbled. He could, he supposed, increase his pace to a gallop and attempt to overtake his quarry before he reached Mesilla. But he chose not to do so. He would follow the Kentuckian into town and stage a showdown there.

Brett Peterson was twenty-four years old and a young man anxious to gain the reputation of being a hot-shot gunfighter. So far he had gunned down no fewer than a dozen men, yet none of them had been renowned as a shootist. To reach the top of his profession and, so, command a high price for the hire of his gun, he needed to take on and gun down a shootist of some distinction. Such a man was Jack Stone and, into the bargain, Stone was an ageing gunfighter, surely no longer as fast as he used to be? Stone would be, Peterson calculated, ripe for the taking.

Four years earlier, a bungled break-in in the city of Chicago had resulted in the death of the householder, a prominent businessman and a member of the city council. Brett Peterson had been one of the gang who broke into the house, and although he had no hand in the actual killing he had nevertheless felt it prudent to flee Chicago and head out West. Since then, he had roamed across the West, earning his living firstly as a bartender, then as a saloon bouncer and ultimately as a hired gun.

Peterson stood one inch short of six foot. Black-haired and sporting a drooping black moustache, he had a hooked nose and long jaw. These features, together with his coal-black eyes, gave him a harsh, vulpine look. His wide-shouldered, sturdy frame was encased in a neat three-piece black suit and white linen shirt, and he sported a black bootlace tie. On his head, at a rakish angle, sat a black derby hat, while on his feet he wore a pair of highly polished black boots. Tied down on each thigh was a black leather holster carrying a pearl-handled forty-five calibre British Tranter, although Peterson, not being ambidextrous, rarely used the revolver on his left hand.

Apart from the white shirt, Peterson was clad entirely in black and, to complete the picture, he had donned a pair of black buckskin gloves and rode a mettlesome black mare. All in all, he presented a dark, menacing figure as he cantered along the Butterfield stage route towards the town of Mesilla.

Ahead of him, Stone crossed the town limits and proceeded slowly down Mesilla's Main Street. It being late afternoon there were few people on the sidewalks and but one wagon and a couple of buckboards rattling along the street. There were, however, several horses tethered to the rail outside

Sweeney's Saloon. In addition to some thirsty towns-folk, a number of cowpokes from the nearby Bar S and Big Valley ranches had ridden into town, aiming to enjoy a few beers at the saloon. Consequently, when Stone pushed open the batwing doors and entered, he found it to be pretty full.

The Kentuckian elbowed his way through the crowd to the bar. Sweeney's was typical of saloons across the length and breadth of the West. It consisted of a double-storey, frame-built building with a rectangular bar-room. A railed walkway ran round the upper level of the saloon, brass lamps hung from the rafters, there were two pot-bellied stoves, neither of which was lit, a couple of spittoons at either end of the marble-topped bar and a large, ornately engraved mirror, which ran the length of the bar-counter. Behind this counter stood Sam Sweeney and his one and only bartender. Both were busily serving the saloon's thirsty customers.

Stone waited his turn and then ordered a beer. He was served by the proprietor, a thin, lanky individual, wan-faced, redheaded and clad in a light-grey three-piece suit. In contrast, the bartender was short and fat, red-faced, and wore a rather grubby white apron over his shirt and trousers.

Having paid for his beer, Stone took it over to a corner table, one of only two still vacant. At the others games of chance were taking place: poker, checkers and blackjack. Stone viewed the busy scene before him, leant back and happily savoured his beer.

Several folk passed in and out of the saloon. Then, some ten minutes after Stone had sat down, the batwing doors swung open yet again, this time to admit Brett Peterson. He had taken a little while to spot Stone's bay gelding among the other horses tethered outside Sweeney's Saloon. He pushed his way through the throng, as Stone had done before him, and eventually reached the bar. While he waited his turn to be served he peered round the bar-room, searching for a sight of the Kentuckian. Eventually he spied Stone sitting and supping his beer at the corner table. He smiled thinly.

This was the moment he had been waiting for. Peterson ordered a whiskey. He downed it in one single draught, then slammed the glass down on to the marbled bar-top and slowly made his way back through the crowd of drinkers to the centre of the saloon. Once there, he weaved between the various tables until he reached the corner where Jack Stone sat supping his beer.

The Kentuckian looked up as Brett Peterson approached his table. His eyes narrowed and his jaw tightened. He sensed trouble.

'Stone?' demanded Peterson. 'Jack Stone?'

'Who's askin'?' growled the Kentuckian.

'Name's Brett Peterson.'

'Never heard of you. Whaddya want with me?'

'I'm told you're pretty fast with a gun.'

'So?'

'So, I reckon I'm a mite faster.'

'That a fact?'

'It is.' Peterson stared hard into Stone's pale-blue eyes. 'An' I intend to prove it,' he added menacingly.

Stone did not trouble to reply; at least, not in words. He simply leant back in his chair and, in one smooth, swift movement, drew his Frontier Model Colt from its holster and fired. Peterson's British Tranter had barely cleared leather when the Kentuckian's first shot struck him in the chest. The second shot drilled a hole in the centre of his forehead and exploded out of the back of his skull in a cloud of brains and blood. Peterson was knocked backwards several feet and was dead before he hit the floorboards.

Confusion reigned for some moments until the crowd of townsfolk and cowpokes realized what had happened. Then a ring of concerned and voluble drinkers and gamblers surrounded the spot where Brett Peterson lay. Their gaze flitted from the corpse on the floor to the Kentuckian sitting at the corner table, calmly supping his beer, with his revolver by now safely back in its holster.

Two figures barged through the crowd and confronted Stone. They were the saloonkeeper, Sam Sweeney, and the town marshal, Jake Draper. In contrast to the thin, lanky, wan-faced Sweeney, Draper was a huge bear of a man, craggy-faced, grey-haired and beetle-browed. He sported a wide-brimmed grey Stetson, a black frock-coat, black velvet vest and dark-grey trousers, and he carried a Remington tied

13

down on his right thigh. His badge of office gleamed brightly on his chest and his harsh features were contorted into a ferocious scowl, while his fierce black eyes glared belligerently at the Kentuckian.

'You jest killed this young buck?' growled the marshal, indicating the inert Brett Peterson with a jerk of his thumb.

'Yup,' replied Stone.

'You got an explanation?'

'It was him or me. He came up an' challenged me.'

'An' why in tarnation would he do that?'

Stone shrugged his shoulders.

'Dunno for sure,' he said.

'Waal, hazard a guess,' snapped Draper.

'Reckon he was out to earn hisself a reputation as the feller who outgunned Jack Stone.'

Draper's eyes widened and there was a gasp from the crowd. Most of those present, including both the marshal and the saloonkeeper, had heard of the Kentuckian and his exploits.

'This happen very often, Mr Stone?' enquired Sweeney curiously.

'Nope.'

This was true, although, as Stone's fame had spread throughout the West, so had such incidents increased. To date three young gunslingers had tried and failed to out-shoot him in an attempt to gain notoriety. Stone feared there would be others in the future.

'How'd he track you here?' demanded Draper.

'Don't rightly know, Marshal. Guess he picked up my trail some place back along the stage route. I first noticed him a few miles north of here. I wasn't absolutely certain he was followin' me until he entered the saloon an' came up to my table an' challenged me.'

'An' then you shot him.'

'I didn't have no choice.'

'No.' Draper frowned and went on, 'We don't tolerate shootin' here in Mesilla. We're peaceable folks an' want our town to stay peaceful. Your kind ain't welcome here, Mr Stone.'

'My kind?'

'Professional shootists.'

'You're a professional shootist, too, Marshal.'

'I'm a law officer an' only draw my gun in the line of duty.'

'So was I mostly when I drew mine. On other occasions, it was drawn purely in self-defence.'

'Even so, your kind are trouble, Mr Stone. An' we don't want no trouble here in Mesilla. So, I'm orderin' you to git outa town.'

'I ain't plannin' on stayin'.'

'Good!'

'But it'll be dark 'fore long an' 'sides, I've had me a hard, dusty ride. Therefore, I aim to spend the night here an' leave town tomorrow mornin'.'

'Now, lookee here . . .' began Draper.

'Aw, come on, Jake,' the saloonkeeper interrupted him, 'it cain't do no harm to allow Mr Stone to stay overnight.'

'Waal, I dunno?'

'I'll leave after breakfast. You got my word on that.'

Although the Kentuckian's tone was conciliatory, Draper sensed that he was not about to back down. And the marshal was, above all else, a pragmatist.

'OK,' he said grudgingly. 'You can stay till after breakfast tomorrow. But no longer. Understood?'

'Understood, Marshal.'

Jack Stone smiled and finished his beer. He had no wish for another confrontation. A few beers, a decent meal and a comfortable bed for the night was all that he wanted. He rose to his feet and headed for the bar, promptly followed by the saloonkeeper. Marshal Draper, meantime, directed one of his deputies, who happened to be in the crowd, to go and fetch the town's mortician.

Thereafter Stone remained at the bar, enjoying a few more beers and conversing with Sam Sweeney and the bartender and various other of the saloon's customers. By the time he eventually left Sweeney's Saloon, the corpse of Brett Peterson had been removed to the funeral parlour and Jake Draper had retired to the law office.

Stone straight away untethered his bay gelding from the rail outside and rode it down Main Street as far as the livery stables, where he left it to be curried, fed and rested. Thereupon, he proceeded to Mesilla's Alhambra Hotel, situated next to the stage line depot and almost opposite Sweeney's Saloon. Here he booked a room for the night and then entered its restaurant and ordered a rib-eye steak, black-eyed peas and fried potatoes, to be washed down with a jug of strong black coffee.

Stone enjoyed a leisurely meal in the congenial ambience of the Alhambra's elegant dining room. By the standards of the time, the hotel was a deal more comfortable and well-appointed than most of those situated in the various townships dotted across the West. He found his bedroom to be of the same high quality as the dining room and, dog-weary after his long ride and his confrontation with Brett Peterson, he retired early to bed and slept soundly through until dawn broke.

Once he had washed, shaved and dressed, the Kentuckian went downstairs and into the hotel dining room, where he intended to partake of a substantial breakfast. It was while he was doing just that that Stone peered out the window and observed the stage bound for El Paso clatter along Main Street and pull up in front of the stage line depot. A change of horses was evidently required, and at the same time, the passengers were taking the opportunity to disembark and get themselves something to eat.

There were five altogether: four men and one young woman, and none was intending to remain in Mesilla. Three were heading for El Paso, the town at the end of the Butterfield stage route, while the destination of the other two was the stage's next port of call, the small desert town of Burro Creek. In the meantime, they all trooped into the Alhambra and seated themselves in the dining room, where they were promptly served since, unlike Stone, their time was limited. Indeed, they had consumed their meals and left before he was three-quarters of the way through his.

He watched them clamber back into the stage-coach. The driver and the shotgun guard had already availed themselves of a quick bite to eat further down the street at the somewhat cheaper Ma Ridley's Eating-house and they were sitting up on the box, ready to depart. Once the last passenger had disappeared inside and one of the depot's staff had slammed shut the stagecoach's door, the driver flicked the reins and set it in motion. Stone observed it clatter past the front of the hotel and, picking up speed, continue on its way along Main Street, heading southwards in the direction of Burro Creek and ultimately its destination, El Paso on the Texas-Mexico border.

Stone had barely finished his breakfast when Marshal Jake Draper marched into the room. He glared at the Kentuckian.

'You still here?' he rasped.

Stone rose slowly to his feet. He had had a good night's rest and a first-rate breakfast and, consequently, he was in a sunny mood. And he had no intention of letting the marshal spoil it.

'Sure am,' he drawled.

18

'Waal, I want you outa . . .'

'Don't git all fired up, Marshal,' replied Stone, with a grin. 'I'm on my way.'

He pushed past the peace officer and headed upstairs to his bedroom, where he intended to retrieve his saddlebags and his Winchester. Then, as he had paid for both room and breakfast in advance, he headed straight past the reception desk and out on to the sidewalk, where he found Draper standing, smoking a large cigar. The marshal said nothing but simply stood and watched Stone as he made his way along Main Street to the livery stables.

A few minutes later Stone was mounted on his bay gelding and trotting through the town in the direction previously taken by the stage. Marshal Draper was by now seated on a rocker on the sidewalk in front of the law office. He continued to smoke his cigar. Stone smiled wryly and raised his Stetson in mocking salute as he rode by. The marshal made no response and Stone rode on, crossed the town limits and then headed out on to the trail.

TWO

While Jack Stone was still making his preparations prior to leaving for Mesilla the stagecoach continued its journey south. On the box were veteran Butterfield Stage driver, Joe Harvey, and his shotgun guard, young Jerry Newton. Harvey, a short, thickset, grizzled fellow, who looked a decade older than his forty-three years, and Newton, a slim, blond-haired twenty-five-year-old, had been working together for almost six years and, so far, had encountered neither bandit nor renegade Indian on any of their many journeys. In consequence, both had become somewhat blasé. Similarly attired in Stetson, brown leather vest, check shirt, denim pants and unspurred boots, each carried a Remington revolver in a holster on his thigh, while Jerry Newton also rested the obligatory shotgun on his knees. Neither man expected to have need of these weapons.

Inside the stagecoach the five passengers had naturally, during the course of their ride, become acquainted.

The three men who were bound for El Paso all headed there for different reasons. Max Gattis, a fat, pasty-faced individual in a black frock-coat and tall stovepipe hat, was due to replace the manager of the town's bank, who was about to retire. The rake-thin fellow sitting next to him and clad in a rather well-worn grey three-piece suit and derby hat was named Tim Morrison, and he was returning from a visit to his ailing mother. The third man, Southern Pacific Railway director Ben Shaw, had been to Tucson on railway business. He lived and worked in El Paso and was attired similarly to Tim Morrison, though his suit was brand new. A rather overbearing and pompous character, of the three he had by far the most to say.

The two who were due to leave the stagecoach at Burro Creek sat side by side opposite the three men.

Edward Tindall had been to Tucson to consult his lawyer regarding the purchase of some land. He was a tall, handsome man in his late forties, but still a bachelor, although recently engaged to a widow who owned Burro Creek's one and only dry-goods store. Tindall was the town's richest man, being sole proprietor of its hotel, livery stables, food and grain store and one of its two saloons, together with several town houses and homesteads from which he derived substantial rents. Indeed, it had been his many business interests that until lately had kept him from seeking a wife.

Like the three men opposite, Tindall was elegantly dressed. He wore a black Prince Albert jacket over a grey brocade vest and fine white linen shirt. He sported a black string tie, immaculately pressed light-grey trousers and highly polished black shoes, and on his head he wore a low-crowned, wide-brimmed black Stetson. With his thick grey-flecked black hair, lofty brow, piercing blue eyes, aquiline nose, firm mouth and strong jaw, and clad in his splendid clothes, Tindall cut a fine and imposing figure.

The young lady sitting demurely beside him was no less striking, for she was extremely pretty in her simple gingham dress and straw hat. Luxuriant glossy chestnut locks framed her lovely heart-shaped face, her large brown eyes sparkled above a retroussé nose that was lightly dusted with freckles, and she possessed a pair of inviting and smiling red lips. All in all, Lizzie Reardon was a delight to look at.

In addition, she was both intelligent and well-educated. Indeed, she was on her way from her home town, Tucson, to Burro Creek, where she was due to take up a post as teacher at the town's fast-expanding school. Consequently, she was only too happy to engage in conversation with Edward Tindall and, by so doing, learn a little about the town in which she was shortly to reside.

Both inside and outside the stagecoach the travellers chatted and relaxed as it clattered southwards towards the next stopping-place, Burro Creek. This part of its route followed the Rio Grande. To the west lay a vast expanse of desert, while to the east were low hills, divided here and there by narrow gulches, and just beyond the hills the river flowed southwards out of sight of those who traversed the Butterfield stage route.

It was some two hours after the stage had left Mesilla when three horsemen suddenly emerged from one of the gulches and formed up across the trail, effectively blocking the stage's passage. All three were masked and clutching revolvers, one Colt Peacemaker and two Remingtons. The man clutching the Peacemaker levelled it at Joe Harvey and yelled at him to halt the stagecoach. Instead, in defiance of this command, Harvey cracked his whip and urged the horses to increase their pace.

This proved to be a fatal mistake, for immediately the horseman aimed and fired. His shot struck Joe Harvey in the chest and knocked him backwards. As he collapsed, Harvey relinquished the reins and the horses veered off the trail. In the same instant, the other two horsemen opened fire, their shots ripping into the guard, Jerry Newton, before he could either draw his revolver or aim and fire his shotgun. He promptly fell off the box and hit the dust, where he lay motionless.

The stage, meantime, was eventually brought to a

halt halfway between the trail and the low hills, which for some miles bordered the Rio Grande. This was accomplished by two of the three masked men riding alongside and grabbing hold of the leading horses' reins.

All three then surrounded the stagecoach, two on one side and one on the other. They were clad so as to remain anonymous. Their garb consisted of plain grey Stetsons, kerchiefs covering the lower half of their faces, ankle-length brown leather coats, black denim pants (mostly unseen) and unspurred brown boots. Their horses were brown geldings, none of which bore any distinguishing markings.

The reason why they wanted to conceal their identity was because they were known locally, since, together with their father, they ran a rather less than successful horse ranch on the edge of Burro Creek. They were the three Docherty brothers: Larry, Danny and Little Billy. Larry and Danny were sturdily built and of about average height while Little Billy, at six foot one inch, was a full four inches taller. He was named *Little* Billy only because he was the youngest. In fact, he was as tall as and as burly as his father, Big John Docherty.

Once they had the stage stationary and surrounded, Larry, the eldest, addressed its passengers.

'OK, folks,' he yelled. 'Git outa the stage on this side. Try climbin' outa the other door an' you're dead.'

Little Billy, who was stationed on the opposite side of the coach, cocked his revolver and added menacingly, 'You better believe it.'

Inside the stagecoach the five passengers collected themselves, having been thrown around when the horses bolted following Joe Harvey's sudden demise. He remained slumped on the box, his shirtfront stained with blood and his eyes staring sightlessly up into the sky. Jerry Newton, meantime, lay where he had fallen, several hundred yards back. And he, too, had breathed his last.

'What . . . what are we gonna do?' quavered a petrified Max Gattis.

'I don't reckon we got no choice,' said Tim Morrison. 'We best do as we're told.'

'I . . . I guess so,' muttered Gattis.

He threw open the door and nervously clambered out. Morrison promptly followed the banker. The railway director, Ben Shaw, was the next to descend from the coach to the trail. Despite the circumstances in which he found himself, he retained his sense of importance and was prepared to address the three road agents accordingly. This he did while Edward Tindall was helping Lizzie Reardon climb down to the ground.

'Now, lookee here!' he cried. 'I am not jest any ordinary common or garden citizen. I am someone to be reckoned with, for I'm a director of the Southern Pacific Railway.'

'Is that a fact?' sneered Larry Docherty.

Shaw bridled and drew himself up to his full height.

'Indeed it is,' he retorted haughtily. 'You harm me an' you will pay for it, believe me. Agents of the Southern Pacific will hunt you down an'. . . .'

But Larry Docherty didn't wait to hear what would happen next. He simply aimed his Colt Peacemaker at the railway director and shot him straight between the eyes.

As Shaw fell backwards and bit the dust his fellow passengers gasped and huddled together. They had expected to be robbed, but not murdered. Now they feared for their lives. And not without reason.

By this time the three brothers were gathered together on the same side of the coach, with their backs to the desert and facing the huddle of frightened passengers. The guns in their hands were levelled at the four of them.

'OK, let 'em have it,' growled Larry Docherty.

Straight away, the three brothers opened fire and all four passengers collapsed in a heap.

An unearthly silence followed the gunfire. The brothers remained for a few minutes surveying the heap of bodies. None moved. Then, satisfied that all of the stage's passengers were dead, they removed their masks.

'What now?' murmured Danny.

'We take all their cash an' valuables an' then hightail it outa here,' said Larry.

'OK. Let's git on with it 'fore someone comes

along an' spots us,' said Little Billy.

Accordingly, he began to dismount, intending to head towards the stagecoach and the pile of corpses. Larry and Danny followed suit. It was while they were in the act of dismounting that Lizzie Reardon suddenly leapt up and sprinted round the back of the coach. She had been brought to the ground, not by one of the fusillade of shots, but by Max Gattis. Hit in both the head and the chest, he had crashed sideways into the girl and knocked her clean off her feet. Consequently, while all three male passengers had been shot, Lizzie, unbeknown to her would-be killers, had hit the ground unscathed. Now she was intent upon making her escape.

Larry Docherty spied her while still in the act of dismounting. He yelled a warning to his brothers and, once he had reached the ground, attempted a shot at the fleeing girl. But he was too late. By the time he had aimed and fired his revolver Lizzie had disappeared round the opposite side of the coach.

'Goddammit!' he rasped. 'Quick, we gotta catch her! The bitch has seen us without our masks!'

Without more ado, the trio ran towards the stage-coach. They rounded it and spotted their quarry approximately one hundred yards ahead of them. They immediately opened fire, but they were no shootists and Lizzie was by now a distant moving target. Their shots failed to hit their mark and they quickly ran out of bullets. Before they could reload their guns Lizzie reached the sanctuary of one of several gulches which cut through the range of low hills bordering the Rio Grande. She promptly vanished into its narrow entrance.

'Holy cow!' cried Larry Docherty in frustration.

He halted, as did his brothers, and, while they reloaded their weapons, they anxiously discussed what to do next.

'We cain't let her escape. She could identify us,' Larry repeated.

'So, she ain't goin' nowhere,' said Danny with a shrug. 'That thar gulch leads straight to the river. She's trapped.'

'Yeah, you're right, Danny,' agreed Larry, relief showing in his rugged features.

'Therefore, we jest follow her down the gulch an' then, sooner or later. . . .'

'We don't all need to go. You an' me, we'll go relieve the corpses of their money an' valuables like Pa told us to. Li'l Billy, you go after the gal.'

'It could be a long walk,' said Little Billy. 'Reckon I'll go git my hoss an' ride after her.'

'Good thinkin',' commented Larry.

So that was how they played it. Little Billy retraced his steps, remounted the gelding and trotted off in the direction of the gulch. At the same time Larry and Danny Docherty prepared to search both the four corpses and the stagecoach for any money or valuables.

*

Lizzie, meantime, hurried on through the gulch. Not being familiar with the locality, she did not realize that she was fast approaching a dead end, that ahead of her lay the Rio Grande.

Breathing hard and with her legs aching, Lizzie rounded one bend after another as she scurried through the narrow, winding gulch. On either side were perpendicular walls of rock. There was no escape route to her right or to her left. She had, perforce, to continue forward.

Her flight ended abruptly and unexpectedly. As she hurtled round the last bend she found she was staring out into space. Indeed, it took her all her time to prevent herself toppling into the abyss that lay ahead of her. She came to a sudden halt and staggered back. Then she stepped cautiously forward and peered down. The gulch ended at a cliff's edge. Beneath her a stretch of rapids tumbled ever onward in a raging torrent.

Lizzie paused, her heart thumping. Above the roar of the rapids she could hear the sound of a horse's hoofs. They were proceeding down the gulch after her. She was trapped. Ahead, lay the rapids. Behind, one of her pursuers was remorselessly approaching.

The girl peered anxiously about her, looking for a crevice in the rock face where she might perhaps hide and avoid discovery. There was none. The cliffs lining the gulch were formed of sheer, unbroken rock. She crept nearer the abyss that lay before her and stared down over the edge. Far below, the waters thundered over rocks. To leap into those rapids would, she reckoned, mean certain death. Yet, should she remain where she was, the fast-approaching horseman would just as surely gun her down.

Standing on the very edge, Lizzie glanced desperately to her left and to her right. Then she saw it: to her right was the narrowest of cracks in the rock face. She had not observed it before because it was in the cliff facing the river and, therefore, out of sight of anyone standing within the gulch. Only by peering out over the river and then sideways had she spotted it. The question was: could she reach the crevice and squeeze into its narrow interior?

Summoning up all her courage, Lizzie flattened herself against the right-hand cliff and edged out over the river, grabbing hold of each and every protuberance, however small, that jutted out from the rock face. Fortunately, the fissure was no more than an arm's length away and, with one last audacious lunge, she succeeded in scrambling into it. In so doing, she lost her hat, which sailed downwards and into the river. Had she not been so slim, Lizzie would not have made it. As it was, she found herself crushed tight between both sides of the narrow opening.

The girl had vanished into the fissure in the nick of time, for, moments later, Little Billy trotted round the final bend. Had he been riding at full gallop, there is little doubt that he would have plunged over the cliff's edge. Indeed, he had to pull hard on the gelding's reins to prevent it from stepping into space. The horse whinnied, its forelegs raised and thrashing wildly. Then Little Billy jerked the reins to one side and brought the gelding to a halt, its front hoofs thumping down safely on terra firma. An inch or two further on, those hoofs would have missed the earth altogether and horse and rider would have surely died. Little Billy breathed a huge sigh of relief and steadied his trembling steed.

Once he had recovered from the shock Little Billy looked around. Where in tarnation was the girl? he asked himself. He carefully studied both sides of the gulch. There was nowhere that he could see where she might have hidden. He glanced down towards the rapids and suddenly spotted Lizzie's straw hat, snagged on a rock. As he watched, the torrent loosened it and swept it away downriver. He grinned.

Little Billy was still grinning as he turned his horse's head and trotted back up the gulch. A minute or two later, he rejoined his brothers at the stagecoach, where they had just finished searching for, and gathering together, their victims' money and valuables.

'Waal,' growled Larry, 'I take it you caught up with the gal an' plugged her?'

'No.'

'No?'

'No, Larry, I didn't need to plug her. That thar gulch ends above a stretch of rapids. I guess she fell over the edge.'

'You guess?'

'Yeah, Larry. I spied her hat floatin' in the water. If'n she was runnin' fast round that last bend, she could easily have plunged over the edge an' down into the rapids. 'Deed, I nearly did so myself. I only jest managed to pull up my hoss in time.'

'Let's go take a look,' said Larry.

'There ain't no need,' protested Little Billy.

'Mebbe not, but I'd like to see for myself. As the eldest, I'm the one who'll be expected to report to Pa.'

'OK. Follow me.'

Little Billy turned his gelding's head and, pursued by his two brothers, headed back along the gulch, although at a much more sedate pace than previously.

Both Larry and Danny carefully and minutely surveyed the rock faces on either side of the gulch. But, like Little Billy before them, they found no possible hiding-place. Eventually, they reached the far end and halted a few paces back from the cliff's edge. Larry and Danny dismounted, then edged cautiously forward and peered down at the raging rapids.

'If'n she landed in them rapids, she's a goner for certain,' opined Danny, with a nod in the direction of the water.

'That's right. She couldn't have survived,' agreed Little Billy.

'Mebbe not,' rasped Larry. 'But I need to be one hundred per cent sure.'

'Whaddya mean?'

'I mean that if by some miracle she did survive, the gal remains a threat.'

'Only if she comes across us face to face,' remarked Danny. 'What kinda description could she give the sheriff? Three tough-lookin' fellers in Stetsons an' long leather coats. Hell, that could apply to almost anybody!'

'Yeah, an' it's not as if we're likely to wear them coats again. Pa went to Silver City to buy 'em for us, specifically for this venture,' stated Little Billy.

'That's true,' admitted Larry.

'An', in the extremely unlikely circumstances that she did survive her fall into the rapids, it ain't likely that we'll ever encounter her again. Since we didn't recognize her, I figure she ain't from Burro Creek or hereabouts. Most likely she was on her way to El Paso,' declared Little Billy.

'That's right,' said Danny. 'An' El Paso ain't some place we'll be visitin'. Certainly not now we're aimin' to leave New Mexico pretty soon an' head for 'Frisco. So, I reckon you don't need to mention 'bout the gal to Pa. We won't say nuthin', will we, Li'l Billy?' he asked.

'Sure won't,' replied Big John Docherty's youngest.

'I dunno?' said Larry. 'If Pa should find out I ain't

given him the full facts. . . .'

'Aw, c'mon, Larry, how in blue blazes can he?' enquired Danny.

'OK. I'll think 'bout what to say.'

'So, can we head back to the ranch?'

'In due course.'

'But. . . .'

'First, we stop off at Sandy Banks. Jest to make sure the gal ain't washed up there.'

'If'n she is, she'll be dead,' said Little Billy.

Sandy Banks was a stretch of the Rio Grande situated a mile or two south of the rapids and just over half a mile outside the town of Burro Creek. It was a pleasant spot where the townsfolk often picnicked and the town's children could swim in safety. Should anyone fall into the rapids and not be trapped under water amongst the rocks, he or she would, in all probability, float downriver and finally surface at Sandy Banks.

'I'm with Larry on this one,' said Danny. 'There ain't no harm in makin' sure.'

Little Billy shrugged his broad shoulders.

'OK,' he said. 'To Sandy Banks it is. An' then, once we've reported to Pa, I say let's head into town, for I sure as hell could murder a beer!'

So saying, he wheeled his horse round and set off at a canter, back the way he had come. Larry and Danny Docherty straight away did likewise and, a few minutes later, all three emerged from the gulch and set off along the trail in the direction of Sandy Banks and Burro Creek.

*

Meantime, inside the crevice, Lizzie Reardon held her breath. She had listened to the receding sound of the horse's hoofs as Little Billy left the scene and headed back towards the plain. As a precaution, she had determined to remain where she was for a few more minutes. Then, just as she was considering leaving her hideout, she heard Little Billy return, together with his brothers. She heard them confer at the cliff's edge, but the thunder of the rapids drowned out their words. She could make out their voices, but not what they said. Then, finally, she heard them turn around and begin to canter off. Only when the sound of their horses' hoofs had completely died away did Lizzie eventually feel it was safe to leave her hideout.

The return from the crevice was no less fraught with danger than the passage to the crevice had been. She scrambled nervously round the corner of the cliff and flung herself on to the floor of the gulch, white-faced, perspiring and panting for breath.

Lizzie lay there for some time while her heart-beat slowed and her breathing returned to normal. Then, somewhat shakily, she rose to her feet and stood listening. Apart from the roar of the rapids, all was quiet. No sound of horses' hoofs broke the silence. Lizzie breathed a huge sigh of relief and took a few tentative steps away from the cliff's edge. Then, still shocked and extremely apprehensive, the girl slowly made her way back along the gulch in the direction of the abandoned stagecoach.

THREE

The stagecoach remained where Lizzie had left it, the horses munching happily on clumps of alfalfa grass. She approached it cautiously and stood beside it, gaping in horror at the three corpses lying in a heap in front of its open door. To one side lay the body of the railway magnate, Ben Shaw, while on the box was that of Joe Harvey and, further back along the trail, the body of the young shotgun guard, Jerry Newton.

Lizzie collapsed to the ground and burst into tears. She continued to weep uncontrollably for some minutes. Then, eventually, she ceased and dried her eyes. She gazed fearfully about her. What if the murderous trio should return? No, she told herself, there was no reason for them to do so. They had presumably robbed their victims of their money and valuables and fled back to wherever they came from. She need only wait for someone to stumble across the scene of the robbery and beg their help.

Then her ordeal would be over.

In a short while her prayer was answered. Lizzie had been sitting there for little more than a quarter of an hour when she spied a lone rider cantering along the trail from the direction of Mesilla. She hastily scrambled to her feet and began waving her arms. The rider, meantime, paused along the way to peer down at the corpse of young Jerry Newton.

As the rider approached her Lizzie blanched and shrank back, for he was a huge bear of a man, with harsh, rugged features, certainly no less intimidating than those of the stagecoach robbers. Lizzie feared the worst, but then he smiled and his countenance lightened.

'Are you OK, miss?' he asked gently.

'Er . . . yes . . . yes; I am unhurt,' she stammered.

'So, tell me what happened,' he said as he proceeded to dismount.

'Well, Mr . . . er. . . ?'

'Stone. Jack Stone.'

The name, which would have been familiar to both peace officers and outlaws across the length and breadth of the West, meant nothing to the young schoolteacher.

'I . . . I was travelling south from Tucson to Burro Creek when the stage was attacked by three masked men,' said Lizzie. 'As you can see, all of my companions were shot dead,' she added with a sob.

'Yeah. Was one of 'em accompanyin' you, or are you travellin' alone?'

'I am travelling alone. My name is Elizabeth Reardon, although family and friends call me Lizzie, and I am on my way to Burro Creek to take up a teaching post.'

'Oh, yeah?'

'Yes. The school there is fast expanding and the schoolmistress, a Miss Violet Peel, required an assistant to start at the commencement of the new scholastic term. An advertisement was placed in the *Tucson Times* and, a few days ago, Miss Peel and the chairman of the school's governors travelled up to Tucson to interview the applicants. There were three of us, from whom I was chosen. Which is how I came to be on board this stage. The new term begins tomorrow.'

'I see.' Stone glanced at the four men lying dead in close vicinity to the coach. 'How come all these folks got shot? Did they offer some kinda resistance?'

Lizzie shook her head.

'No,' she said. 'After the driver and the guard were shot, the robbers pursued us and eventually succeeded in bringing the stagecoach to a halt. They then ordered us to get out and simply gunned us down.'

'But you survived.'

'I . . . I was lucky. Mr Gattis' – here she indicated the fat banker lying sprawled in front of the stage – 'was hit and, as he collapsed, he fell against me and knocked me flat. The robbers didn't realize this. They must've assumed they'd killed us all. So, I waited until they were in the act of dismounting and then I made a run for it. I ran round behind the coach and sprinted across the plain towards that gulch over yonder. The robbers chased me and shot at me, but missed. And I managed to reach the gulch and vanish into its interior.'

'Didn't they pursue you into the gulch?'

'Oh, yes!'

'Then, how in tarnation did you elude 'em?' asked the Kentuckian, as he surveyed the short range of hills and the various gulches cutting through them. 'Surely you must've reached a dead end, for don't all them passages through the hills terminate at an' above the Rio Grande?'

'I imagine they do,' replied Lizzie. 'The one I took certainly did.'

'Then. . . ?'

'I found a crevice in which to hide.'

'An' your pursuers overlooked it?'

'Yes.'

'They must've been darned unobservant.'

'Not really. You see, it was not in either of the rock faces lining the gulch. It was in that which overlooked the rapids and, therefore, quite difficult to pick out. Also, I was wearing a hat, which I lost when I clambered into the crevice. The hat fell into the rapids, where I believe it was spotted by one of my pursuers.'

'Who jumped to the wrong conclusion, Miss Reardon?'

'Exactly, Mr Stone.'

The big Kentuckian grinned broadly.

'Waal, luck's surely been on your side,' he drawled. 'You ain't Irish by any chance?'

Lizzie smiled.

'No, Mr Stone, I am not.' The smile faded and she continued in a low voice, 'Sadly, the others didn't share my luck.'

'No.'

'Why didn't they just rob us? Why did they have to try to kill us all? It doesn't make sense. They were masked and, so, unrecognizable.'

'Yeah.'

'I suppose Mr Gattis, Mr Tindall and Mr Shaw might have been carrying a decent sum of money on their persons, But I wasn't and I doubt if Mr Morrison was either. To hold up the stage and carry out those murders for so little gain!'

'As you said, it don't make no sense.'

'It does not.'

'But, then, the fellers who did this are evidently a bunch of cold-blooded killers. I figure they gunned down your companions jest for the sheer hell of it. An' if'n they were masked as you said . . .'

'They were when they opened fire on us.'

Stone glanced quizzically at the young school-teacher.

'What are you sayin', Miss Reardon?' he asked.

'Afterwards, thinking we were all dead, they removed their masks,' said Lizzie.

'You . . . you'd recognize 'em if you saw 'em again?' he said keenly.

'Yes, Mr Stone, I would.'

'Can you describe 'em?'

'They were big, burly men, tough-looking and I'd say in their mid to late twenties. They had no distinguishing features, scars or suchlike, that I recall, yet I would definitely be able to identify them should we meet.'

'How were they dressed?'

'Pretty plainly, I'm afraid. Grey Stetsons and long brown leather coats.'

'The weather bein' warm an' springlike, I reckon the coats were worn as part of their disguise. I don't s'pose they normally wear 'em, 'cept in winter.'

'No.'

'Waal, now they're long gone. However, the sheriff in Burro Creek is sure to have a pile of Wanted posters. Mebbe you'll be able to pick 'em out?'

'Perhaps?'

'Anyways, let's git you to your destination. I daresay Miss Peel will be wonderin' what's become of you, for the non-arrival of the stagecoach must've caused some comment in town. Folks will be askin' what's delayed it.'

Lizzie looked about her and shuddered.

'What . . . what about my fellow-travellers and . . . and the driver and the guard?' she enquired tremulously.

Stone smiled warmly at the girl.

'I'll . . . er . . . settle them inside the coach, an' that way, we'll transport 'em into town.'

'But. . . ?'

'You can ride up front with me.'

'Oh, yes, of course! Thank you,' said Lizzie relievedly. For just one moment she had envisaged herself sharing the stage's interior with half a dozen corpses.

Stone remounted his bay gelding.

'I'll go fetch the shotgun guard,' he said.

'Can . . . can I help you in any way?' asked Lizzie, although the very thought of touching any of the dead bodies filled her with dread.

'No; you jest stay put till we're ready to roll,' replied Stone.

It took the Kentuckian some time to carry the body of Jerry Newton from where he lay to the stage-coach. He heaved the youngster's corpse inside and propped it up on the seat immediately behind the box. Then he fetched Joe Harvey's body from the box and sat it next to Jerry's. Thereafter, he went to each prostrate passenger in turn and conveyed them to the coach. Tim Morrison he placed inside next to the driver and the guard, while the other three he propped up on the seat opposite.

'Waal, miss, I figure we can now head on to Burro Creek' he said, as he shut the stagecoach door.

'Y . . . yes, that would be good, Mr Stone,' replied an ashen-faced Lizzie.

'Let me help you up on to the box.'

'Thank you.'

'Are you OK? You're tremblin'.'

'It . . . it's the shock. I shall be all right, Mr Stone, once we reach the town.'

'It's only 'bout two or three miles south of here,' said Stone reassuringly. 'We'll soon be there.'

He turned and went to tie his bay gelding by its bridle to the rear of the stagecoach. Then he joined the girl on the box, lifted the reins and set the stage in motion.

'Are you, like me, heading for Burro Creek?' enquired Lizzie.

'No. I'm on my way to Texas, to sign up for the cattle drive that each year proceeds north from San Antonio to Julesburg in Nebraska.' Stone smiled and continued, 'I was in Mesilla when this here stage rolled into town.'

'Were you indeed?'

'Yup. I was havin' breakfast in the Alhambra's restaurant.'

'But we all disembarked and went there for *our* breakfasts!' exclaimed the girl.

'I know. I observed you enter an' leave.'

'I didn't notice you, Mr Stone.'

'No, in common with your fellow travellers, you were concentrating on your meal.'

'We hadn't much time. We needed to finish it before the horses were changed and the stage was ready to resume its journey.'

'Exactly. I, on the other hand, was in no partickler hurry. So, I had the opportunity to observe all the other folk in the restaurant.' Stone grinned and added, 'An' I sure as hell wasn't about to overlook an attractive young lady like you.'

Lizzie's ashen features were suffused by a blush and a timid smile momentarily displaced the look of shock and sadness which had previously pervaded the girl's pretty young face.

'You flatter me,' she said diffidently.

'I don't reckon so,' replied Stone. 'Heck, you'll find yourself beset with admirers once you're settled in Burro Creek! You jest see if you ain't.'

'Well, I don't know,' murmured Lizzie.

' 'Course you will. An' that'll help take your mind off what happened out here on the trail.'

'Eventually it might, I suppose. However, I imagine that first of all I shall be expected to relate everything I heard and saw to the local sheriff.'

'Yup. 'Fraid so.'

'I had best concentrate my mind so that I achieve total recall,' said Lizzie, furrowing her brow as she made the effort.

'Yes, miss,' said Stone.

It was while the young schoolmistress and the big Kentuckian were thus engaged in conversation that the stagecoach rattled past a fork on the river side of the trail. This fork led straight to Sandy Banks, upon the edge of which the Docherty brothers had dismounted and were now standing, idly smoking cheroots. A small stand of cottonwoods screened the fork from the sight of those travelling south until the very last minute. Consequently, neither Lizzie or Stone observed the three brothers, although Little Billy chanced to turn as the stage sped by and he spotted Lizzie Reardon sitting up on the box beside the Kentuckian.

'Holy cow!' he cried. 'That was the stage that's jest gone rattlin' past!'

'What!' exclaimed Larry Docherty in alarm, and almost swallowing the remains of his cheroot.

'But, how in blue blazes. . . ?' began Danny.

'It was bein' driven by some big feller in a Stetson an' a buckskin jacket,' said Little Billy.

'Waal, I s'pose this here feller was ridin' south an' chanced upon it. Sooner or later somebody was sure to . . .' speculated Larry, as he calmed down a little.

'That ain't all,' Little Billy interrupted him.

'Whaddya mean?' growled Larry.

'Sittin' up on the box beside the big feller was that gal we figured had fallen into the rapids.'

Larry Docherty gasped and turned his gaze back towards the river. He and his brothers had been standing for quite some time at the edge of the water, gazing upriver from Sandy Banks. Seeing no sign of the girl, they had naturally concluded that she had drowned and was trapped beneath the rocks that formed the rapids. Nevertheless, they had stood there awhile, in case her body should break free and float on down to Sandy Banks. Now they were confronted with the astonishing fact that she was alive. Larry could scarcely believe it.

'How is this possible?' he demanded. 'There was no way she could've hidden from us in that gulch. The sides were composed of sheer, unbroken rock.'

'I swear it was her,' reiterated Little Billy.

'But, how. . . ?'

'Never mind how,' said Danny. 'If'n Li'l Billy's right, then it is darned lucky we didn't ride straight into town. Should we have done an' afterwards come face to face with the gal, she would've denounced us for sure.'

Larry nodded and frowned.

'We need to know whether Burro Creek's her destination,' he growled.

'If it is . . .' Danny looked grim.

'We are in deep trouble,' Larry finished his brother's sentence for him.

'So, what are we gonna do?' asked Little Billy anxiously.

'We head back to the ranch an' tell Pa everythin',' said Larry. He bestowed a searching stare upon his father's youngest. 'Are you certain sure the gal you saw on the stage is the same one you chased up that thar gulch?' he demanded of Little Billy.

Little Billy met the other's stare without flinching.

'I'm certain,' he said firmly.

'OK, let's git goin', then,' declared Larry.

The three brothers tossed their unfinished cheroots into the water, left the river's edge and hurriedly mounted their horses. Moments later they were galloping hell for leather towards the horse ranch, which lay half a mile to the east of Burro Creek.

FOUR

The arrival in town of the stagecoach, with Lizzie Reardon and Jack Stone up on the box in place of the shotgun guard and the driver, caused both surprise and consternation amongst Burro Creek's citizenry. As the stage crossed the town limits and rattled up Main Street, they poured out of their business premises, stores and houses and scurried after it until Stone brought it to a halt before the stage-line depot.

Sheriff Lew Flood rose from the rocking-chair on the sidewalk in front of the law office, which happened to be situated next door to the depot, while his young deputy Frank McCoy, who had just returned from his morning's circuit of the town, approached the stage from the opposite direction. The two lawmen met beside the stage, backed by a crowd of curious townsfolk. The mayor, Hiram C. Lancaster, pushed his way through the throng to join the peace officers. He called up to the

Kentuckian, 'What're you doin' up there? Where in blue blazes are Joe Harvey an' young Newton?'

Jack Stone did not reply immediately. Firstly, he ran his eye over the trio, observing them closely. Hiram C. Lancaster had about him the air of an aristocrat, with his tall, elegant frame and lofty demeanour, and in his expensive black derby hat and frock-coat. Lew Flood, too, possessed an air of authority. He was a big, tall, broad-shouldered man in his mid-forties, his hair flecked with grey and his face weather-beaten and lined. He was attired in a grey Stetson, check shirt, brown leather vest and faded blue denims. His badge of office was pinned to the vest and he carried a Colt Peacemaker in a holster strapped to his right thigh. Frank McCoy was similarly armed and clad, although his Stetson was black and low-crowned. Only twenty-two years old, the deputy remained full of youthful zeal and vigour, his handsome young countenance bright and eager-looking. All of this Stone observed and noted. Finally, he responded.

'Would you be the mayor of this here town?' he enquired of Lancaster.

'I certainly would. Hiram C. Lancaster at your service. Now, 'bout Joe Harvey an' . . .'

'Take a look inside the stage, Mr Mayor.'

'What. . . ? I . . . er . . . I. . . .' Lancaster peered in through the stagecoach door. 'Jeeze!' he cried. 'It's plumb full of corpses!'

The sheriff and his deputy stepped up beside the

mayor and followed his gaze. Frank McCoy paled, a look of shock stamped across his young face.

'Go fetch Saul Barnaby,' Sheriff Flood instructed him.

'Yes, Sheriff. Right away, Sheriff,' replied the deputy and he hurried off towards the nearby funeral parlour.

'An' tell him there's six dead bodies to deal with,' Flood shouted after the departing deputy. Then he turned his attention to the Kentuckian. 'Sheriff Lew Flood,' he announced. 'An' you are. . . ?'

'Jack Stone. An' this young lady is Miss Lizzie Reardon. She was on her way here to take up the post of schoolteacher when the stage was held up an' all her fellow passengers were murdered. Shot down in cold blood.'

'Oh, you poor, poor dear! What a terrible experience! You must have been terrified!' exclaimed a voice from the crowd and a short, stocky, grey-haired woman in a plain brown dress and bonnet forced her way through the crowd. 'Let me get you home at once,' she added firmly.

'Hold your hosses, Miss Peel,' growled Flood. 'I got some questions I need to ask both Mr Stone an' the young lady 'fore you whisk her away.'

'But, Sheriff . . .' Violet Peel began to protest.

'It . . . it's all right, Miss Peel,' said Lizzie to the schoolmistress she had come to Burro Creek to assist, and in whose house it had been proposed she should reside.

'I won't keep you long, miss,' said Flood, as he handed the girl down from the coach. He turned to Violet Peel and stated, 'I intend to do my questionin' in the privacy of the law office. So, if'n you'd care to accompany Miss Reardon. . . ?'

'I most certainly would,' replied Violet, and, taking hold of Lizzie by the arm, she marched up on to the sidewalk ahead of both the sheriff and Stone.

'I'd appreciate it, Lew, if you'd let me sit in on this,' said Lancaster.

'Of course, Hiram.' Flood threw open the law office door and ushered the two ladies inside. Then, spying Frank McCoy returning across the street accompanied by the mortician, Saul Barnaby, he called out, 'The corpses are all sittin' up inside the stage, Saul. I'll leave it to you to take 'em an' lay 'em out in the funeral parlour. You, Frank, come an' join us in the law office.'

'Yes, Sheriff,' said Frank, relieved that he was not to be involved in the gory business of removing the half-dozen bodies from the stagecoach to Saul Barnaby's place of business.

Once the six were inside the law office and all seated round the sheriff's large mahogany desk, Lew Flood introduced his deputy to Jack Stone and Lizzie and then began his interrogation.

'OK, Miss Reardon,' he said, 'jest take your time an' explain exactly what happened.'

'Yes, Sheriff. It . . . it was like this . . .' began Lizzie. She then proceeded to describe the events from the moment the Docherty brothers appeared on the scene and attempted to hold up the stagecoach. She had arrived at the point where, following the shooting of the driver and the shotgun guard, the stage was eventually brought to a halt and the passengers ordered to dismount. At this juncture, however, Lizzie was interrupted by a loud knocking on the law office door, and a highly agitated Saul Barnaby burst in on them.

'Sheriff,' he cried, 'did you take a good look at them there corpses inside the stage?'

'No, I confess I didn't,' said Flood. 'Did you, Hiram?'

'N . . . no. I'm afraid I averted my gaze jest as quick as I could,' said the mayor.

'Me, too,' added Frank McCoy, his youthful features paling at the memory.

'So, you didn't manage to identify any of 'em?' said Barnaby.

'Nope,' replied the sheriff.

His deputy and the mayor said nothing, but merely shook their heads.

'Waal, you'll be shocked to learn that one of the corpses is that of our esteemed deppity mayor an' fellow citizen, Ed Tindall.'

Hiram C. Lancaster gasped. He and Edward Tindall had long been the best of friends. Between them they owned most of the town's businesses. Yet this had not led to rivalry, for whereas Lancaster had taken an active interest in local politics, Tindall had not. He was a businessman pure and simple, and it had required all of Lancaster's powers of persuasion to convince his friend that he should accept the position of deputy mayor. In Tindall's hands it had been no more than an honorary post. And so the two had complemented each other, remaining both Burro Creek's leading citizens and, at the same time, boon companions. And now, suddenly that friendship was ended. Lancaster could scarcely believe that his friend was dead. He slumped forward, his head in his hands.

'Oh, my God!' he sighed. 'Who's gonna tell Emma an' young Sidney?'

'Who are you talkin' about?' asked Stone.

'Emma Younger. She's a widow an' owns Burro Creek's only dry-goods store. She an' Ed became engaged a coupla weeks back.'

'An' Sidney?'

'He's Ed's nephew. Sidney Bailey. He works for his uncle. Has done 'bout ten years. They've always been pretty darned close.'

'I see.'

'I'll break the news to Mrs Younger,' offered Violet Peel.

Stone observed that, whereas Sheriff Flood had referred to the widow by her Christian name, the schoolmistress did not. Violet Peel was, he concluded, someone who preferred to preserve the formalities.

'An' I'll inform Sidney,' said Flood.

'Thanks,' said Lancaster. Turning to the mortician, he asked, 'Are there any other of our citizens amongst the dead?'

Saul Barnaby shook his head.

'No, Mr Mayor,' he replied. 'I didn't recognize anybody else.'

'I think I can enlighten you, Sheriff, as to the identities of the other passengers,' said Lizzie quietly.

'Indeed?' said Flood.

'Yes. During the course of our journey we all introduced ourselves and got to know a little about each other.'

'OK. Pray go on, Miss Reardon.'

'Well, they were all bound for El Paso. Mr Tim Morrison was returning home after visiting his ailing mother in Tucson. Mr Max Gattis was on his way to El Paso in order to replace the manager of the bank, who was due to retire. And Mr Ben Shaw had been to Tucson on railway business. He claimed to be a director of the Southern Pacific Railway.'

'Would you be prepared to step across to the funeral parlour an' identify which is which?' Flood enquired of the young schoolmistress.

'Oh, you can't ask the poor dear to do that!' exclaimed Violet Peel. 'After all she's gone through, it would be too distressing.'

Lizzie smiled gratefully at her soon-to-be superior.

'It's all right, Miss Peel,' she murmured.

'No, it is not, Miss Reardon,' stated Violet.

'No . . . well, anyway, I feel I owe it to them. They were very pleasant travelling companions and to die like that . . .' Lizzie dissolved into tears.

'Now look what you've done, Sheriff,' said Violet angrily.

Lew Flood did not respond immediately. He waited while Lizzie composed herself and dried her eyes.

'It ain't essential,' he said. 'It's jest that I figured if'n we knew who each was, we could label the coffins accordingly 'fore we send 'em to either El Paso or Tucson.'

'Yes, of course,' said Lizzie.

'So, whaddya say?'

'Yes, I shall accompany you to the funeral parlour, Sheriff,' she stated.

'And I shall come, too,' said Violet firmly.

Again Lizzie smiled gratefully at the older woman. While it seemed that Violet Peel was one to observe the formalities, nevertheless it was also clear to Lizzie that Violet had a kind heart. She would, Lizzie felt sure, prove to be a supportive colleague and a good friend.

'OK,' said Flood. 'That's settled. We'll see you there later, Saul.'

'Sure thing, Sheriff,' said the mortician. He promptly left the law office and headed back across the street to the funeral parlour.

Having apprised Lew Flood that Edward Tindall was one of the dead, he needed his assistant's help to transfer the six bodies from the stagecoach to his premises, there to lay them out. Subsequently, he expected to have to convey five of them by hearse to either El Paso or Tucson.

Meantime, back in the law office the sheriff had asked Lizzie to resume her narrative.

She obliged, telling her audience how, by a stroke of luck, she had not been shot down by the three road agents and how, while they were in the process of dismounting, she had succeeded in running off and reaching the gulch in which she had found a hiding-place. During the course of this narrative Lizzie also mentioned that the hold-up men had removed their masks and later, at the far end of the gulch and immediately above the rapids, stood awhile talking. She concluded by relating how, once they had ridden off, she had returned to the stagecoach, where she was found by Jack Stone.

'Thank you, Miss Reardon, that was most informative,' said Flood.

'It sure was,' agreed Stone. 'But I guess you may wanta pose a few questions, Sheriff?'

'I do, Mr Stone,' said Flood. He smiled at the girl. 'If'n you wouldn't mind, Miss Reardon?'

'No, not at all,' said Lizzie. 'Please feel free to ask me anything you want.'

'OK. Firstly, you said there were three men who held up the stage. Can you describe 'em?'

'They were wearing Stetsons and long leather coats. But I don't suppose that helps much?'

'Nope. However, you said they removed their masks.'

'Yes.'

'Waal, can you describe their faces?'

'Not really. I didn't properly study them. I was in too much of a hurry to escape.'

'Even so.'

'I'd say they were in their late twenties or early thirties, and tough-looking.'

'Any distinguishing features? A scar mebbe, or a broken nose, or. . . ?'

'Not that I noticed.'

'Hair colour? Blond? Red-headed?'

'I'm not absolutely sure, but, as far as I can recall, I think all three had brown hair.'

'Were they short? Tall? Medium height?'

'Again I'm not sure. I ran off as they were dismounting and I couldn't see them from my hiding-place in the gulch. The crevice in which I was sheltering looked out over the river. Which is why they didn't spot it.'

'But you did hear them talkin'.'

'Yes, Sheriff.'

'What were they sayin'? Did you mebbe catch a name?'

Lizzie shook her head.

'No,' she said sadly. 'I could hear them speaking, but I couldn't make out what they were saying. The sound of the rapids drowned out their words.'

Sheriff Lew Flood slumped back in his chair. He

had hoped that perhaps Lizzie might have been able to provide him with a clue as to the killers' identities.

'You could show Miss Reardon our pile of Wanted notices,' suggested Frank McCoy.

Flood favoured his young deputy with a smile.

'Yeah, Frank. Good idea.'

There were one or two posters stuck upon the walls both inside and outside the law office. However, Flood kept a complete set in his desk drawer. He fished these out and placed them on the table in front of the girl. Lizzie pulled her chair forward and began, slowly and meticulously, to study each poster in turn. This took some considerable time, yet to no avail.

'I am pretty certain none of these men was involved in the hold-up,' she said finally.

'Goddammit!' exclaimed Flood.

'So, what do we do now?' asked Frank McCoy.

'I s'pose we'd best head on out to where the stagecoach was held up an' see if we can pick up those varmints' trail. Can you show us where you found the stage, Mr Stone?'

'I guess so, Sheriff,' replied the Kentuckian.

Flood eyed his deputy speculatively.

'One of us will needs remain in town. Somebody's gotta be here to maintain law an' order. We cain't both go ridin' off,' he remarked.

'No, sir,' said Frank.

Stone frowned. Since Lew Flood was sheriff and not marshal, his jurisdiction related not merely to the town of Burro Creek. It extended to the entire county of which Burro Creek was presumably the county seat. Therefore, surely, Stone assumed, he employed more than just the one deputy?

'Ain't you got no other deppities?' he demanded.

'We sure have, Mr Stone,' replied Flood.

'Waal, then?'

'I got three others, but they're out huntin' Apaches.'

'Apaches? But I thought the Apache wars ended when Geronimo surrendered?'

'They did.'

'So?'

'Since then, from time to time, we git a bunch of young bucks lettin' off steam. They leave their reservation an' go on the rampage, stealin' hosses an' cattle an' generally makin' a nuisance of theirselves. Usually, these break-outs occur in the spring. Sometimes it's the Jicarilla, sometimes the Mescalero. This spring it's a band of Chiricahua braves led by a young hothead named Chaco.'

'The Chiricahua are, I take it, from around these parts?'

'They are, Mr Stone.'

'So, this is your problem?'

'Yup. Like I said, I got three deppities on the look-out for 'em.'

'An' how do these spring sorties usually end?'

'It depends. Mostly there's no bloodshed an' either the young bucks simply quit their games an' head back to their reservation, or their chief sends out a few elders to track 'em down an' fetch 'em back. On the rare occasions when some white man is killed defendin' his stock, then the US Army steps in an' the offendin' Apaches are hunted down an' shot or taken an' hanged.'

'An' your three deputies?'

'Oh, there ain't no chance they'll catch Chaco an' his young bucks! But we gotta show willing. Hell, we cain't jest sit back an' let 'em ride roughshod across Dawson County!'

'I s'pose not.'

'No. Anyways, I've spoken to their chief. He's gonna let 'em indulge their high spirits for a li'l while longer and then, if'n they don't return to the reservation of their own free will, he'll dispatch some of his best braves to track 'em down.'

'Assumin', in the meantime, they don't kill nobody.'

'Jest so.'

'It all seems a waste of manpower. Them three deppities—'

'Are needed here.' Flood shrugged his shoulders and continued, 'I know, but, over the last few weeks Chaco an' his pals have run off quite a number of cattle an', as a result, the ranchers are gittin' mighty fed up. They are expectin' me to do somethin' about it, an' I'm hopin' the deppities' presence out on the range will mebbe help keep those darned Apaches at bay an' outa trouble.'

'You don't sound too confident.'

'No.'

Hiram C. Lancaster smiled slyly and interjected, 'Lew ain't got no choice, Mr Stone. Y'see the election for sheriff comes up this November an' he cain't afford to alienate the ranchers, not if he wants to git hisself re-elected.'

Flood smiled wryly.

'That's about it,' he confessed. 'Anyways, let's forgit the Apaches for now an' git back to this business of them murderin' road agents.'

'Yeah. Mr Stone was offerin' to take one of us out to the scene of the hold-up,' said Frank McCoy. 'So, which of us is it to be, Sheriff?'

'I guess it had best be you, Frank,' replied the sheriff. 'I'm needed here in town.'

The young deputy grinned.

'Let's git goin' then,' he said eagerly.

'Jest one thing, Frank,' said Flood. 'You git on the trail of them varmints, you do exactly what Mr Stone tells you.'

'But I'm the deppity!' protested the youngster.

The sheriff smiled and patted Frank on the shoulder.

'The name Jack Stone don't mean nuthin' to you, does it?' he said.

'No, Sheriff, it don't,' replied Frank.

'Waal, it does to me.' Flood turned to the Kentuckian and said, 'I was kinda preoccupied earlier, so didn't git around to sayin' I'm real pleased to meet you. This here feller's a legend of the West, Frank; the man who tamed Mallory, the roughest, toughest town in all Colorado.'

'Is that so?'

'It is, Frank. So, you do as I say an' listen to Mr Stone. OK?'

'Yessir.'

'Good! Now, Mr Stone . . .'

'Call me Jack.'

'Right, Jack. D'you want I should deputize you?'

'I don't think that'll be necessary, Sheriff.'

'OK. Waal, if you're both ready to ride?'

'I'll jest saddle up my hoss,' said Frank.

So saying, the youngster promptly hurried out of the law office, closely followed by the Kentuckian. This left the sheriff, the mayor and the two ladies. The sheriff rose from behind his desk.

'Shall we step across to the funeral parlour?' he asked quietly.

Lizzie nodded and immediately Violet took hold of her arm. Flood crossed the office and held open the door. He followed them outside, where they took their leave of the mayor. He, for his part, felt in need of a stiff drink and consequently headed down the street towards the Hot Spurs Saloon.

The others crossed the street to Saul Barnaby's funeral parlour. Here an ashen-faced and rather tearful Lizzie Reardon identified the bodies of the three men bound for El Paso. Then she and Violet departed, walking slowly arm in arm in the direction

63

of Emma Younger's dry-goods store.

'I'll see to it that your portmanteau is taken off the stage an' delivered to Miss Peel's house. Jest as soon as I've spoken to Ed Tindall's nephew,' promised Flood.

'Thank you, Sheriff,' replied Lizzie.

Violet eyed her concernedly and said, 'Do you mind if we call in on Mrs Younger to break the dreadful news?'

'N . . . no, that's all right. Of course you must do that,' responded Lizzie.

'We won't stay long. Then I'll get you home and make you a nice cup of tea,' declared Violet.

Lizzie smiled gratefully.

'That would be lovely,' she said.

'And, although the new school term commences tomorrow, you needn't take up your duties immediately. In the circumstances—'

'No,' said Lizzie. 'I should like to start work straight away. It will help take my mind off those dreadful killings.'

'Of course. Just as you like.'

They continued on their way along Main Street and soon reached Emma Younger's establishment. They went in and found her alone behind the counter.

Lizzie was surprised to observe that Edward Tindall's fiancée was nowhere near as old as she had expected. She had taken Tindall to be in his late forties and had assumed that Emma Younger would be of a similar age. But this was clearly not so. It was evident to Lizzie that the widow was in either her late twenties or very early thirties.

'Hullo, Miss Peel.' Emma greeted the schoolmistress with a ready smile.

'Good morning, Mrs Younger,' replied Violet, grim-faced, her tone solemn.

'Is . . . is something the matter?' asked Emma, suddenly anxious.

Violet nodded.

'I'm afraid there is, my dear. Please prepare yourself for a shock,' she said sombrely.

While Violet was quietly informing Emma of the death of her fiancé, Sheriff Lew Flood was busily searching for Edward Tindall's nephew. Sidney Bailey could genuinely be described as a Jack-of-all-trades. He was a bright, intelligent young man who had, during the decade he had worked for his uncle, proved himself invaluable. In addition to taking control of the day-to-day running of Tindall's hotel, he had helped prepare the accounts for each of his other businesses and, once a month, had collected the rents from Tindall's many tenants.

Flood eventually ran Bailey to ground in the hotel's wine cellar, where the young man was occupied in compiling an inventory. He guessed that Bailey took after his father in looks, for he most certainly did not in any way resemble his late uncle. Small, dark-haired, thin-faced and of a pallid complexion, Sidney Bailey was no Adonis. Although not actually ugly, he could scarcely be described as hand-some. He was, in fact, a rather nondescript thirty-year-old. His clothes, however, did afford him some degree of elegance. As hotel manager, Bailey was clad in a splendid black Prince Albert coat and light-grey velvet vest, a fine white linen shirt with ruffled collar, a grey silk cravat, immaculately creased dark-grey trousers and highly polished black leather shoes.

He looked up as the sheriff entered the cellar.

'Howdy, Sheriff. You lookin' for me?' he asked.

'Yup,' replied Flood.

'So, what can I do for you?'

'Nuthin'.'

'Nuthin'?'

'Nope. I've jest come to give you some news.'

Bailey eyed the sheriff warily. It was clear from the look on his face that Lew Flood was not about to impart good news.

'Tell me,' he said.

'I'm afraid the stagecoach on which your uncle was travellin' back to Burro Creek was held up,' said Flood.

'Held up? What . . . what happened?'

'Three armed robbers stopped it 'tween Mesilla an' here. They gunned down everyone on board: the driver, the shotgun guard an' all the passengers 'cept one.'

' 'Cept one?'

'Yeah. By a miracle she escaped unscathed.'

66

'She?'

'A Miss Reardon. She's come to Burro Creek to help Miss Peel run the local school,' explained Flood, adding, ' 'Deed, she's lodgin' with Miss Peel.'

'An' jest how did this Miss Reardon manage to survive?' enquired Bailey.

'It was like this . . .' The sheriff went on to describe the hold-up, the cold-blooded killings and Lizzie's lucky escape, just as Lizzie had related them to him.

While he was talking Sidney Bailey plonked himself down on a wine barrel and stared wide-eyed and open-mouthed at Flood. Then, no sooner had Flood finished than he asked grimly, 'You got any idea who those murderin' varmints are, Sheriff?'

Lew Flood shook his head sadly.

'Nope,' he said. 'I showed Miss Reardon my pile of Wanted notices, but she didn't recognize anyone.'

'But she *did* see the killers?'

'Yeah. Like I told you, thinkin' everyone was dead, they removed their masks.'

'So, she would recognize 'em if she saw 'em again?'

'Sure would. But that ain't likely, Sidney.'

'You reckon not?'

'My guess is they're a bunch of desperadoes who slipped across the line from Texas or some other adjoinin' state, or mebbe even across the border from Mexico.' Flood sighed. 'If'n I'm right, I figure they'll have slipped back an' are long gone, never to return.'

'Hmm, I s'pose. A bad, bad business, Sheriff. Jeeze, to think that Uncle Ed is dead! I can hardly believe it!'

'I'm afraid it's true, Sidney. What I cain't understand is, why in blue blazes did they shoot all those folks? There was no need. They could've simply robbed 'em of their money an' valuables an' then headed off back to wherever they came from.'

'I agree. But surely some outlaws are like that? They kill for the sake of killin'.'

'That seems to be the only possible explanation,' concurred Flood, although, in truth, he was not entirely convinced by this argument.

'Poor Uncle Ed!' exclaimed his nephew.

'D'you wanta see him?' asked Flood.

The young man hesitated. Then he rose up from where he had been sitting on the wine barrel.

'I ain't lookin' forward to this, Sheriff,' he said. 'But I . . . I feel I oughta.'

'Let's go, then,' said Flood.

He turned and, followed by Sidney Bailey, made his way up the stone steps that led into and out of the wine cellar.

FIVE

The horse ranch could hardly be described as flourishing. It had originally been jointly run by Big John Docherty and his brother, Michael. Michael had been the one who knew about, and truly cared for, horses. While he lived the ranch had prospered. His death, five years earlier, had marked the beginning of its decline. Then, the demise of Big John's wife two years later had made matters worse. Since that sad event Big John and his three sons had spent more and more time carousing and whoring in the Hot Spurs Saloon and less and less working the ranch. None of them possessed Michael Docherty's knowledge of horseflesh and, accordingly, their stock had deteriorated. As a result they had lost several contracts including their most profitable: the one to supply horses to the US Army at Fort Thorn. In consequence, the ranch was barely breaking even and Big John Docherty was currently two months in arrears with his rent.

He was an older version of his youngest son, Little Billy. Six foot one inch of muscle and bone, the rancher presented a formidable figure. Fierce black eyes peered out from a harsh, rugged face, the bottom half of which was covered by a thick black beard. His attire was that of the average cowboy: Stetson, check shirt, leather vest, Levis and boots, while in his holster Big John carried an Army Model Colt.

He was in the corral in front of the ranch house, checking the left foreleg of a particularly broken-down grey mare, when he heard the thunder of horses' hoofs. Looking up, he observed his three sons riding hell for leather across the plain towards the ranch. He abandoned the mare and, carefully closing the gate behind him, left the corral and went to meet his sons. They pulled up their horses at the foot of the flight of wooden steps leading up to the ranch house porch and hastily dismounted.

'Let's go inside,' said Big John.

He clattered up the steps and into the ranch house. The others followed and, once they were all inside, Big John produced a bottle of whiskey and four glasses, which he proceeded to fill. He handed one glass to each of the brothers.

'Thanks, Pa,' said Larry, as he accepted the whiskey.

'OK. Gimme your report,' growled his father.

'First, let me git outa this goddam coat. It's makin' me as hot as hell,' said Larry.

'Me, too,' echoed Danny and Little Billy simultaneously.

Big John waited impatiently while the three divested themselves of the long leather coats. Then, once they had done so, he rasped, 'OK. Git on with it!'

Larry nervously cleared his throat, took a slug of whiskey and began.

'We held up the stage like you told us to, Pa,' he said. 'We shot the driver an' the shotgun guard, an' we ordered all the passengers to step outa the coach. Then we gunned 'em down.' He paused and added hesitantly, 'Waal, nearly all of 'em.'

'Nearly all of 'em!' roared Big John Docherty. 'What in tarnation d'you mean?'

'He means that one got away,' said Danny.

'One got away! Who, goddammit?'

'A gal. Dunno who she is. She was lined up with the rest of 'em an' when we opened fire, she went down with the others,' said Larry.

'We thought they'd all been shot, but I guess she was mebbe knocked over by one of the others fallin' against her,' explained Little Billy.

'That's right. Which is how she missed gittin' shot,' added Larry gloomily.

'That so?' Big John glared at his three sons. 'Didn't you think to check that they was all dead, you lunkheads?' he demanded.

' 'Course we did, Pa,' said Larry.

'The gal, she got up an' ran away while we was still

dismountin' an' 'fore we could start checkin',' stated Little Billy.

'That's right. She dodged round behind the stage-coach an' ran off towards that range of low hills borderin' the Rio Grande, then she disappeared down a gulch an'—' continued Danny.

'I know them gulches. They all end high up above the river. There's a long stretch of rapids,' Big John interrupted him.

'You got it, Pa,' said Larry.

'So, you had her trapped.'

'We thought so.'

'Whaddya mean, you thought so?'

Larry stared uncomfortably at his feet, studiously avoiding his father's furious gaze. Then, slowly and with some reluctance, he related how Little Billy had pursued their quarry to the gulch's far end and had spotted her straw hat floating down below in the rapids, subsequently to be swept away. He went on to describe how he and Danny had also ridden to the gulch's end and how, as a precaution, all three brothers had scoured the gulch's steep sides for any sign of a possible hiding-place, but had found none. He concluded by confessing, 'The thing is, Pa, she *did* escape, God knows how!'

'We rode on to Sandy Banks, thinkin' that mebbe the gal's body might have been swept downriver an' got washed up there,' said Little Billy.

'An' had it?' growled Big John.

'No, Pa. We was there, down by the riverside

havin' a smoke, when I chanced to look round an' see the stagecoach pass by on its way to Burro Creek. There was some big guy drivin'. He'd presumably been on his way south from Mesilla an' jest come across it.' Little Billy paused and added dejectedly, 'Sittin' up on the box beside him was the gal we'd chased into that danged gulch.'

'Jeeze! That beats all! She must've been hidin' someplace that you numskulls overlooked!' exploded Big John.

'I . . . I think I know where. It jest came to me,' declared Little Billy.

His two brothers stared at him in stupefaction.

'Where the heck. . . ?' gasped Larry.

'We scoured both sides of the gulch like you said. But what we didn't scour was the cliff faces over-lookin' the river. If'n there was a crevice close by one or other side of the gulch, mebbe the gal could've scrambled round an' into it?'

'That would've been a mighty dangerous thing for her to do,' commented Larry.

'Sure, but if she was desperate enough . . .'

'I s'pose.' Larry scratched his head. 'Yeah,' he conceded finally. 'I guess that's what she must've gone an' done. It's the only possible explanation.'

'So, boys, we got us a survivin' witness to your hold-up,' rasped Big John. 'Therefore, it's jest as well that you was masked,' he remarked.

'But we weren't,' murmured Danny.

'What!'

'Y'see, Pa, when the shootin' was over, we figured they was all of 'em dead an' we lowered our kerchiefs,' Danny explained.

'You did what?' yelled Big John.

'The gal could only have had a quick glimpse at us 'fore she ran off,' said Larry.

'A quick glimpse?'

'Yeah, Pa. I doubt she'd recognize us again.'

'Do you, Larry? Waal, I wouldn't bet on it. She ain't gonna forget your ugly mugs in a hurry.' Big John studied each of his sons in turn. Luckily, he thought, none of them bore a scar or other distinguishing feature. Nor would the girl have necessarily taken them for brothers, since Little Billy took after him whereas the other two took after his late wife's family and were not particularly alike. 'When you was all three of you in that gulch, I guess you spoke together?' he growled.

'Yes, Pa,' said Larry.

'Did you mebbe address each other by name or say anythin' that could help identify you?' asked Big John sternly.

'Even if we did, that gal wouldn't have heard us. The sound of the rapids was so goddam loud I could barely hear what Larry an' Li'l Billy was sayin', an' I was standin' right next to 'em,' stated Danny.

'Yeah, that's right, Pa,' agreed Larry. 'She would've been too far away to have heard our exact words.'

Big John thought long and hard. He remained

furious that his sons had been careless enough to let the girl escape. However, he felt somewhat reassured by what they had just told him. It seemed that, unless the girl met them face to face, they would be safe enough.

'This gal. You said you didn't know who she is,' he remarked.

'Yeah. We ain't never seen her before. She ain't from round these parts,' said Larry.

'OK. So she could've been on her way to anywhere along the trail, El Paso mebbe?'

'Guess so, Pa.'

'Therefore, providin' her destination wasn't Burro Creek, we ain't got nuthin' to worry about,' said Little Billy with a grin.

'No, for we ain't plannin' on visitin' El Paso nor any other town hereabouts,' added Danny.

'Hell, no! It's 'Frisco here we come!' cried Larry cheerfully.

'When we git our money,' growled Big John. 'In the meantime, you boys will remain on the ranch. Burro Creek is outa bounds while that gal remains there.'

'But if she's on her way to El Paso . . .'

'We don't know that, Larry.'

'So, we jest stay here coolin' our heels?'

'Yup.'

'For how long?'

'I dunno. A li'l while yet, I guess. I'm gonna head into town, find out what I can 'bout the gal you lunkheads failed to shoot dead, an' then see what the situation is regardin' the money that's owin' us. Like you boys, I can hardly wait to start our new life in 'Frisco.'

'Yeah, Pa. An' the money an' valuables we got from the hold-up will sure come in useful once we git there,' commented Danny.

'Every li'l helps, but it's peanuts compared to what's comin' to us,' retorted Big John.

The three brothers nodded. What their father said was true.

'While you're gone, we'll add up the dollars an' collect together the valuables in one big pile,' said Larry.

'Yeah, you do that.'

So saying, Big John went to saddle his horse. By the time he had done so, his sons had heaped all their loot on to the kitchen table. They then stepped outside on to the porch and watched him ride off.

'OK, let's go count them dollars,' suggested Little Billy as their father vanished round a bend in the trail.

They retraced their steps and gathered round the table. However, before they began to deal with the stolen cash, Larry refilled their glasses, emptying the whiskey bottle in the process. All three thirstily threw back the amber liquid.

Big John Docherty, meantime, headed on towards the town, and a few minutes later he had covered the half-mile between the ranch and Burro Creek and was riding down Main Street. Anxious to appear his usual self and to give no clue that he knew about the hold-up, Big John did what he normally did on entering town. He tethered his horse to the rail outside the Hot Spurs Saloon. Then he clattered up on to the sidewalk and strode into the bar-room.

The Hot Spurs was like countless other saloons situated in towns across the West. Like Sweeney's Saloon in Mesilla, it consisted of one large rectangular bar-room. However, it was practically deserted. This was not surprising since the hour was not yet noon. Apart from the bartender and four of Burro Creek's regular topers, only Hiram C. Lancaster was present. He was enjoying his second whiskey of the morning when Big John joined him at the bar.

' 'Mornin', Mr Mayor,' Big John greeted him.

' 'Mornin', Big John; can I offer you a drink?' enquired the mayor genially.

'Thanks, Hiram. A beer, if you please,' replied the rancher.

'I reckon I'll have me another whiskey,' said Lancaster, hastily gulping down the remains of his dram. 'Set 'em up, Al,' he instructed the bartender.

Al obliged and, when the pair had sampled their respective drinks, Big John asked casually, 'So, what's new in town?'

Lancaster stared at the rancher.

'I take it you ain't heard?' he murmured.

'Heard what, Hiram?'

' 'Bout the hold-up.'

'What hold-up?'

'The hold-up of this mornin's stage.'

Big John shook his head, a contrived look of surprise etched across his face.

'No, I ain't heard nuthin' 'bout that,' he said. 'Hell, I've been on the ranch all mornin' an' you're the first feller I've spoken to since I hit town! So, tell me what happened?'

'It was like this,' began the mayor, and he went on to describe in detail the arrival of the stagecoach driven by Jack Stone, the arrival, too, of the one surviving witness to the hold-up, the discovery of the six corpses inside the stage and the subsequent conference in the law office.

'Deppity McCoy an' Mr Stone have gone out to the scene of the hold-up, to see if they can pick up the tracks of them murderin' bandits,' he concluded.

'Let's hope they can,' declared Big John, although, in truth, he hoped the opposite. Since his sons would have ridden along the Butterfield stage route on their way to Sandy Banks, he reckoned it would be difficult, if not impossible, to pick out the prints of their horses' hoofs from those of the many others which had travelled that same trail. 'You said that the survivor, Miss Reardon, actually saw the bandits' faces,' he remarked.

'Yup. But her description was too vague for the sheriff to identify 'em. An', 'sides, they didn't feature on any of his Wanted notices,' replied Lancaster with a sigh.

'That's a pity. But how is Miss Reardon, by the way? She must've been real shook up,' said Big John, injecting a note of concern into his voice.

'I think she'll be OK. Miss Peel has taken her under her wing.'

'Miss Peel?'

'Yes; Miss Reardon was on her way to take up the post of Miss Peel's assistant.'

'She's a schoolmistress?'

'Yup.'

'An' she's to stay here in Burro Creek?'

'Naturally, since she's gonna teach at the local school.'

'Of course. Waal, I hope this ain't put her off none.'

'I don't think so, Big John. She seemed quite ready to take up the post. I figure she'll prove a real asset to this town.'

'Oh, good!'

Lizzie Reardon's appointment posed an unexpected problem. Big John had hoped that her destination was anywhere other than Burro Creek. Now he badly needed to think and to consult.

Thinking and consulting, however, were for the moment denied him, since, at this juncture, Sheriff Lew Flood pushed open the batwing doors and stepped into the saloon.

He joined the other two at the bar, whereupon Lancaster proposed a fresh round of drinks. Once these had been poured and the three had consumed a first draught of their respective beverages, Flood informed his companions that he had just broken the news of Edward Tindall's death to his nephew.

'Sidney seemed real upset,' he concluded sombrely.

'That young man will have much to attend to,' commented the mayor.

'Waal, 'course, there's the funeral an'—'

'Saul Barnaby an' the Reverend Jones will likely sort that out between 'em. No, it's Ed's various business affairs that'll need young Sidney's attention,' remarked Lancaster.

'Hell, yes! There's gonna be quite a few changes, I reckon. For a start, you'll have a new landlord, Big John,' stated Flood.

'Guess I will at that,' replied the rancher. He lifted his glass and threw back the rest of his beer, then slammed the glass down on to the bar counter. 'I think I'll jest go offer my condolences,' he said. 'Where is he, by the way?' he enquired of the sheriff.

'We parted at the funeral parlour an', last I saw, he was headin' in the direction of the hotel,' said Flood.

'Thanks.'

Big John left the other two still drinking at the bar and ambled out of the saloon. Minutes later he found Sidney Bailey at his office in the Burro Creek Hotel.

At that same moment Jack Stone and Deputy Frank

McCoy arrived at the scene of the morning's hold-up. They dismounted and walked their horses along the gulch down which Lizzie Reardon had earlier fled. On the way, both to and from the gulch's furthest point, Stone several times knelt down and studied the various hoofprints. Then, once they had returned to the spot from whence they had started, Frank McCoy turned to the Kentuckian and asked, 'Did you learn anythin' from studyin' them thar marks, Mr Stone?'

The Kentuckian shook his head.

' 'Fraid not, Frank,' he said. 'I was hopin' that mebbe one or other of the horseshoes would have somethin' to distinguish it from the rest. But there was nuthin' I could see, no nick or other kinda defect.'

'So?'

'So, I ain't gonna be able to pick out the hoofprints of the bandits' hosses from those of the other folks ridin' up an' down the Butterfield stage route.'

'Oh!'

'If they've stuck to the main trail, there ain't no way I can tell whether, followin' the hold-up, they headed north towards Mesilla or south towards Burro Creek.'

'Then, ridin' out here was a waste of time?'

'Mebbe, mebbe not.'

'Whaddya mean, Mr Stone?'

'On our ride back to town, we keep our eyes peeled for any sign of hoofprints veerin' off the trail

81

an' out across the plain. We're lookin' for three sets.'

'An' if we spot 'em?'

'We follow 'em, Frank.'

Stone smiled wryly and climbed back into the saddle. Frank McCoy followed suit and they turned their horses' heads and cantered back down the trail, southwards towards Burro Creek.

SIX

Big John Docherty tapped forcefully on the office door, thrust it open and stepped into the office. This consisted of a small square room, three walls of which were lined with wooden cabinets. The fourth side was mostly window and this looked out on to Main Street. In front of the window sat Sidney Bailey. His back was to it and he was poring over a pile of documents, which were strewn across a large mahogany desk. He looked up as Big John barged in.

'I figured we'd better talk, Sidney,' said Big John, and he pulled up a chair on the opposite side of the desk to the young hotel manager and businessman.

Sidney Bailey regarded the rancher with a less than friendly eye.

'I should've thought it wise for us not to talk,' he retorted. 'Surely we oughta keep our distance, at least for the time bein'?'

'Why in tarnation shouldn't we talk?' rasped Big

John. 'It's perfectly natural that I should drop in an' offer you my condolences. After all, your uncle was my landlord.'

'Yeah, an' you are two months in arrears with your rent,' said Bailey.

'Which fact is known only to me an' to you.'

'That's so.'

'But I didn't call jest to discuss my rent.'

'No.'

'Things didn't go exactly to plan.'

'You're darned tootin' they didn't. From what Sheriff Lew Flood told me, I'd say your boys sure messed up.'

'They were unlucky.'

'They were careless.'

While Big John agreed with Sidney Bailey, he was not about to admit as much. He had not come to discuss what had happened, but rather what to do next.

'Look,' he said, 'the main thing is: your uncle's dead.'

'I s'pose.'

' 'Course it is. You're his sole survivin' relative. You'll inherit everythin'. Hell, you're gonna be a mighty wealthy man!'

'Looks like.'

'Thanks to me an' the boys.'

'I'll grant you that.'

'The boys gunned him down jest like we planned. 'Fore he could marry the Widow Younger an' make out a will in her favour.'

'They were also s'posed to gun down all of his fellow passengers.'

'Yeah, that was what they aimed to do but—'

'I don't want no excuses. Uncle Ed's business trip to Tucson was a godsend. When I last called on you to collect the rent we were both in big trouble. You were two months in arrears an' couldn't pay, an' I had jest heard that, after all these years as a bachelor, Uncle Ed had gone an' got hisself engaged to Emma Younger. I'd worked for him from the age of twenty an' it was understood I'd inherit when he was dead, for wasn't I the son he'd never had? But now it seemed quite likely he would, after all, produce an heir. An' where would that leave me? Which is how I came to invite you an' your sons to participate in my li'l scheme.'

'Participate! Goddammit, it was us who were to carry it out! You was takin' no active part an', therefore, bearin' no risk whatsoever.'

'No, but I was gonna pay you well for the risk you were takin'. Five thousand dollars. More than enough to set you all up in business someplace else. Where did you say you intended goin'?'

' 'Frisco.'

'Leavin' behind a failin' horse ranch an' two months' unpaid rent. That was the bargain.'

'Yeah.'

'An' no suspicion would fall on either me or you regardin' his death. It would be assumed that Uncle

Ed was simply one of the hold-up gang's several victims.'

'That still is the case.'

'Yes, but, as Sheriff Flood informed me, we now have a live witness, someone who saw your boys an' would recognize them. What, in blue blazes, induced them to remove their masks?'

'They thought all the passengers were dead.'

'Waal, they thought wrong.'

'Yeah. Which is why I'm here. Did the sheriff tell you that the witness was headed here, that she's gonna be teachin' school an' is residin' with Miss Peel?'

'He did.'

'So, what are we gonna do?'

'I don't rightly know, Big John.'

'We cain't jest do nuthin'. The plan was for us to let a few weeks pass an' then, when folks had more or less forgotten 'bout the hold-up, you'd pay us the five thousand dollars an' we'd sell off our stock, leave the ranch an' move on. Nobody then would have any reason to connect our departure with either the hold-up or your uncle's death.'

'So?'

'That plan won't work. Durin' the few weeks we remain here, we are s'posed to carry on as usual so as not to attract any suspicion. If we was to start actin' outa character, folks might wonder why.'

'Then don't act out of character.'

'You want us to ride into town, pick up our supplies from Hank Reid's general store an' frequent

86

the saloon jest the same as we've always done?'

'Waal. . . .'

'There's hardly a day passes when me an' the boys don't step into the Hot Spurs.'

'I realize that, Big John.'

'Then realize this: sooner or later that li'l schoolmistress is sure to run into us.'

'Not if you restrict your saloon visits to the late evenin'. She ain't likely to be walkin' the streets after dark.'

'But up till now we've dropped into the Hot Spurs at various different times of night and day. An', anyways, what about pickin' up our supplies? There's always at least two of us callin' at the store, usually me an' Li'l Billy.' Big John scowled darkly and declared, 'There ain't no way we can carry on the same as before, not without the boys riskin' bein' recognized.'

'You could call at the store either mid-mornin' or early afternoon, when Miss Reardon is occupied with her teachin',' suggested Bailey.

Big John emitted a short, sharp, humourless laugh.

'We gotta pass the school on our way into town,' he rasped.

'So?'

'So, Sidney, if'n Miss Reardon should choose to look out the window or, for some reason, step outside—'

'OK! OK! I take your point,' conceded Bailey.

'Then I repeat my earlier question: what are we gonna do?'

Sidney Bailey scratched his head.

'I dunno,' he said morosely.

'Waal, I cain't keep the boys corralled up at the ranch for ever more.'

'No.'

'Mebbe for the next coupla days? I could, I s'pose, tell anyone who asked that they was busy roundin' up some hosses that had run off.'

'That would certainly buy us a li'l time,' said Bailey, brightening slightly.

'Yeah.'

'In the meantime, we both must try an' think of somethin'. For starters, I'll go round an' call on the two ladies, see if I can gain Miss Reardon's confidence.'

Big John Docherty nodded.

'Yeah. An' while you're doin' that, I'll discuss the problem of the schoolmistress with Larry an' the other two. Also, you'd better begin gatherin' together the pay-off you owe us.'

'The plan was to wait awhile 'fore I handed over the five thousand,' protested Bailey.

'If we cain't solve our li'l problem, me an' the boys will have no choice other than to vamoose pronto an' take a chance whether our doin' so sets folk talkin'. Hell, they won't necessarily link our departure with the hold-up!'

'No, but they might, an' I don't figure it's a risk

worth takin',' remarked Bailey. ''Sides, five thousand dollars is a lotta loot. I aimed to slowly accumulate the cash over a period, raidin' this account an' that account, sellin' off this asset an' that asset, doin' nuthin' too obvious that might alert either my uncle's bankers or his business associates.'

'Hmm, that's all fine an' dandy, Sidney, providin' we come up with a solution to our problem. Otherwise . . .' Big John left his sentence unfinished, but Bailey got the message.

'I'll do my best to speed things up,' said the young hotelier. 'However, I won't be able to start proceedings until after the will is read an' the inheritance is legally mine.'

'That could prove awkward.'

'I realize that, Big John, but that's the way it is. Let's both see what we can come up with an' meet for further discussion sometime tomorrow.'

'When an' where d'you suggest?'

'If one of us comes up with somethin', then he contacts the other straight away. Otherwise we meet here at, let's say, six o' clock tomorrow evenin'. OK?'

'OK. For now, I'll head on back to the ranch.'

'An' I'll pay that call upon Miss Reardon.'

The two men left the hotel together. Big John crossed Main Street and untied his horse from the rail outside the Hot Spurs Saloon. He mounted and rode off in the direction of the horse ranch. Sidney headed in the same direction, though he proceeded on foot. Eventually, he reached a small, neat, one-storey red brick house, its garden surrounded by a white-painted picket fence. He pushed open the wooden gate and walked briskly up the narrow path to the front door. Then he composed himself before tapping on the door.

The door was opened by Miss Violet Peel. She looked surprised to see him, which was natural enough, since he had never before called upon her.

'I . . . er . . . I thought I'd call upon Miss Reardon an' . . . er . . . pay my respects,' he explained hesitantly.

'Of course. Do come in, Mr Bailey,' replied Violet.

'Thank you, Miss Peel.'

Bailey removed his hat and followed the schoolmistress through to a small sitting room, where evidently the two ladies had been enjoying a cup of tea together. Lizzie Reardon rose from her chair as the young man entered the room.

'Good afternoon, Miss Reardon. Let me introduce myself. I am Sidney Bailey, Mr Edward Tindall's nephew,' he stated quietly.

'Oh, good afternoon, Mr Bailey!' she responded.

'Pray do sit down,' said Violet to their visitor.

'Thank you.'

The two ladies resumed their seats and Bailey found himself a chair.

'Would you care for a cup of tea?' enquired Violet.

'Er . . . no, thank you, Miss Peel,' said Bailey. 'I jest wanted to call and find out how Miss Reardon was bearin' up after her dreadful ordeal.'

'Reasonably well, thank you,' said Lizzie and, glancing gratefully at her hostess and fellow teacher, she added, 'Miss Peel has been so very kind and made me feel quite at home.'

'Good! I am glad to hear it. I hope that what happened will soon become a distant memory and you will settle down to a full and happy life here in Burro Creek,' declared her visitor.

'I hope so, too,' said Lizzie. 'But, of course, you must have been terribly shocked to learn of your uncle's death.'

'I was indeed.'

'You have my sincere condolences, Mr Bailey.'

'And mine,' said Violet Peel.

'Thank you, ladies. I confess it will take me a long time to recover from my grief, for Uncle Ed and I were very close,' commented the young man.

'Let us pray that the miscreants who carried out that murderous attack on the stagecoach are soon captured and brought to justice,' remarked Violet.

'Amen to that,' said Bailey solemnly.

'Yes,' said Lizzie, adding, 'It was very thoughtful of you, Mr Bailey, to call to see how I was feeling.'

'Waal, I know that I am still in shock, and it must have been so much worse for you bein' involved in the hold-up and darned nearly gettin' shot.'

'Yes, it was terrifying.'

'The sheriff told me that those desperadoes removed their masks and you saw their faces. He said you would recognize 'em if you saw 'em again.'

'I certainly would. Although I only glimpsed them before I fled, their features are forever engraved upon my brain.'

'Not that you are likely to see them again,' said Violet. 'I imagine that, by now, they have either bolted across the state line into Texas or across the border into Mexico.'

'Yes. More than likely,' agreed Bailey. Privately, he wondered what on earth he could do to prevent some future confrontation between Lizzie and Big John Docherty's three sons. 'I . . . I'd best be going,' he said. 'I jest wanted to let you know, Miss Reardon, that my thoughts are with you. I hope that you will soon be able to put this entire distressing incident behind you.'

'Thank you, Mr Bailey. I shall endeavour to do so,' replied Lizzie.

'Good! Waal . . . er . . . may I perhaps call again? I should very much like to treat you ladies to tea at my hotel.'

'Yes, of course. That would be very nice,' said Lizzie politely, although, in fact, there was something about Sidney Bailey that she found vaguely disquieting. She could not, however, have said exactly what it was and she had no wish to deprive Miss Peel of the chance of tea at the hotel.

Violet, for her part, was pleased that the young man had taken the trouble to enquire after her new colleague and, as Lizzie suspected, was not at all disinclined to sample tea at the Burro Creek Hotel.

'Good afternoon then, ladies,' said Bailey.

'Good afternoon, Mr Bailey,' said Lizzie.

'I'll see you to the door,' said Violet.

This the schoolmistress proceeded to do, and a few minutes later Sidney Bailey found himself outside the house and walking back down the path to the street. His mention of tea at the hotel had been made up on the spur of the moment, without his having any clear idea how that would help solve his problem. He could, he supposed, slip some poison into Lizzie Reardon's tea. He shrugged his shoulders. The very idea was laughable, yet he had no other cogent plan for eliminating the one and only witness to the Docherty brothers' crime. Deep in thought, he turned and set off up Main Street towards the hotel.

His departure from Violet Peel's neat red-brick house did not go unobserved. As the front door closed behind him Jack Stone and Deputy Frank McCoy crossed the town limits on their way back from visiting the crime scene.

En route Stone had noted two places where travellers had left the main trail. The first was the fork leading to Sandy Banks and the second that leading to Big John Docherty's horse ranch. Both had signs of horses passing to and fro, though Stone could not positively identify any of them as belonging to the horses ridden by the killers of Edward Tindall and the others. The young deputy had, however, informed him as to where the hoof marks led.

Now Frank McCoy exclaimed as he spotted Sidney Bailey turn out of the schoolmistress's gate: 'Goddammit, seems Ed Tindall's nephew's been callin' on Miss Peel an' Miss Reardon!'

'What's his name again?' enquired Stone.

'Sidney Bailey.'

'Hmm. Waal, I s'pose he jest called to ask how Miss Reardon is feelin' after her ordeal.'

'Yeah, I guess so.'

'He's Mr Tindall's heir, ain't he?' surmised Stone.

'He is. When Ed Tindall's widowed sister died 'bout ten years back, he invited Sidney, his only livin' relative, to come stay with him. An', from that time on, Sidney has worked for his uncle. He's a pretty smart feller by all accounts an' has been real useful to Mr Tindall. His main job is managin' the Burro Creek Hotel, but I'm told he's also helped out with the book-keepin' an' has collected the rents from some of his uncle's tenants. 'Deed, that hoss ranch we passed earlier is run by one of Mr Tindall's tenants.'

'An' did Sidney Bailey collect the rent from that partickler tenant?'

'Yup.'

'I b'lieve you said it was run by a certain Big John Docherty an' his sons?'

'I did. Larry, Danny an' Li'l Billy. Though, from what I hear, the ranch ain't doin' too well.'

'No?'

'Nope.' Frank McCoy glanced back at Sidney Bailey, whom they had overtaken as they trotted along Main Street towards the law office. 'There was talk of Mr Tindall mebbe havin' to evict 'em. Now that task'll fall to Sidney.'

As he spoke, they reached the law office and dismounted. Once they had hitched their horses to the rail outside they entered the building and found Sheriff Lew Flood seated behind his desk.

He looked up and asked, 'How'd it go?'

Stone shrugged his brawny shoulders.

'The three bandits' hoofprints merged with all the others on the Butterfield Stage Route. I looked for any sign of them veerin' off, either out on to the plain or up into the hills, but there was none,' he said. 'Consequently, I cain't say whether they headed north or south along the trail.'

'There were various hoofprints leadin' off down the forks to Sandy Banks an' to Big John Docherty's place,' remarked the deputy.

'But there ain't no reason to suspect any of these were left by the bandits. Lots of folk seem to have visited both Sandy Banks an' the hoss ranch,' said Stone.

'So, we ain't no further forwards?' sighed Flood.

'No, Sheriff, we ain't,' confessed the Kentuckian.

'What do we do now?' asked Frank.

Sheriff Flood scratched his head.

'I dunno,' he said. 'I've telegraphed every peace officer in this an' the surroundin' counties with a description of the no-account critters. Don't know what else any of us can do.'

'What about your other three deppities? Cain't you contact them an' ask 'em to temporarily abandon their search for those young Apache bucks you spoke of an', instead, start lookin' for the desperadoes who held up the stage?' suggested Stone.

'My deppities could be jest about anywhere. Until they return to town, I ain't got no idea as to their whereabouts,' replied Flood.

'I s'pose me an' Mr Stone could ride out an'—' began Frank McCoy.

'No, Frank. Your chances of stumblin' across those desperadoes are too darned slim. My guess is they've hightailed it outa Dawson County an' are miles away by now,' said Flood. 'What d'you reckon, Jack?' he asked.

The Kentuckian smiled wryly.

'I'd say that's likely,' he concurred.

'So, we jest do nuthin'?' said Frank McCoy, frowning and looking decidedly dejected.

'That's right. We've got enough on our hands keepin' law an' order here in Burro Creek. Therefore, unless we git word that them desperadoes have been spotted elsewhere in the county, we remain in town.'

'If you say so, Sheriff.'

'I do, Frank.' Flood turned to the Kentuckian and asked, 'How about you, Jack? Are you plannin' on stayin' around awhile, or are you headin' on out?'

'I ain't in no danged hurry to git to San Antonio,' responded Stone. 'I figure I'll stay here in Burro Creek for a coupla days, jest to see what, if anythin', transpires. An', in the meantime, I'm gonna git me a nice cool beer. You care to join me, Sheriff?'

Lew Flood shook his head.

'No, Jack, 'fraid not. Had me a beer a li'l while back, in company with our mayor an' Big John Docherty. Now I got duties to attend to.'

'Mebbe later on?'

'Yeah. Drop in here later this evenin'. If things are quiet, I'll git young Frank to mind the office while you an' I enjoy a few beers at the Hot Spurs.'

'I look forward to it.' Jack Stone smiled and, raising his Stetson, said, ''Afternoon, Sheriff. 'Afternoon, Deppity.'

Then he promptly quit the law office, crossed the street and made his way to the saloon. He pushed open the batwing doors and headed towards the bar-counter, where he found Hiram C Lancaster still standing drinking, exactly as the sheriff had left him earlier.

SEVEN

Chaco and half a dozen other young Apache bucks galloped across the plain in the direction of Big John Docherty's horse ranch. Their spring madness had lasted for some weeks, during which time they had raided several ranches in Dawson County and around Burro Creek, and had run off both cattle and horses. They had also become aware of the three deputies dispatched by Sheriff Lew Flood with instructions to apprehend them, and had led the trio a merry dance into and through the surrounding hills. So far, the Apaches had deliberately shot over the heads of any pursuing ranchers, for their aim was to make a nuisance of themselves, rather than to kill anyone. And Chaco proposed that their intended raid on Big John's horse ranch should be their last.

Chaco, at nineteen, was the oldest of the seven Apaches and a nephew of the Chiricahua chief. He was a bright and intelligent youngster and realized that it was time to draw their rampaging to a close. They had had their fun and, should they prolong their raids much longer, they would in all likelihood provoke the chief into sending some of the tribe's elders to track them down and fetch them back to the reservation. This, Chaco knew, would displease his uncle, who, while he tolerated his young bucks occasionally letting off steam, expected them to know when to stop and to return of their own volition.

Riding at the head of the small band of Apaches, Chaco cut a commanding figure. A tall, handsome youth, with shoulder-length black hair and proud, aquiline features marked with black war paint, he rode his small, tough black pony at a steady gallop. He wore a faded brown shirt, a black leather belt, a white breechcloth and buckskin boots; he carried a Colt Peacemaker in a holster and a bone-handled knife in a sheath, both attached to the belt at his waist. His rifle, a Winchester, he carried in his left hand. His comrades were similarly clad and armed.

Their approach was completely unnoticed by the occupants of the horse ranch, for all three Docherty brothers remained at the kitchen table, still drinking whiskey. They had lumped the valuables, which they had taken from the corpses of their hold-up victims, into one pile and had counted the money. This they had laid in separate heaps, each depending on denomination and whether it was in the form of notes or coins. Then they had concentrated on the whiskey. The brothers were on to their third bottle when Chaco and his band threw open the gate to the first of the ranch's two corrals and released the horses. It was the Apaches whooping and firing their rifles into the air as they chased the horses out on to the plain, that alerted the brothers.

Little Billy was the first to stagger to his feet. But he failed to reach the door, for in his haste he caught his foot behind one of the table legs and sprawled full length across the kitchen floor. As for Larry and Danny, they crashed into each other as they attempted to throw open the door of the ranch house. At the second attempt, they succeeded and stumbled out on to the porch, first Larry and then Danny. They struggled to draw their revolvers, but, before they could fire them, they were driven back indoors by the Apaches' rifle-shots, which slammed into the lintel above their heads. As the two brothers dived through the doorway they ran into Little Billy who, by this time, had managed to clamber to his feet. This collision, however, brought all three of them to their knees.

Outside, meanwhile, the Apaches had emptied the corral and were intent on driving the horses away from the ranch, across the plain and towards the distant hills. In the lead was Chaco, delighted with the success of this, their final sortie. His delight, however, was to be short-lived. He had not observed that Naches, the youngest of the braves, was riding hell for leather in the opposite direction, heading straight for the second corral situated just in front of the ranch house.

Naches had been named after one of the Chiricahua Apaches' greatest warriors and the sixteen-year-old was determined to live up to his name. He aimed to single-handedly release and drive off the horses in the second corral. Had he only had the three Docherty brothers to contend with, he would undoubtedly have succeeded. But, unfortunately for him, it was at this very moment that Big John Docherty chose to return to his ranch.

The rancher was a hundred yards or so away when the Apaches began whooping and shooting off their rifles. His mind was busily engaged in contemplating what to do about Lizzie Reardon's presence in Burro Creek. All such thoughts, though, were banished the second those shots rang out. Big John immediately urged his horse forward and, drawing his rifle from his saddleboot, set off at full gallop towards the ranch house.

As he rounded the house, the rancher spotted Naches in the act of throwing open the gate to the corral. Straight away, Big John raised the Winchester, clamped it to his shoulder, took aim and fired. The bullet struck Naches in the side of the head, penetrating his brain. The young buck was dead before he hit the ground. Big John galloped across and made sure the gate was shut so that none of the horses inside could escape. Then he dismounted and examined the fallen Indian. Having ascertained that Naches was indeed dead, Big John made to rise when he was struck by a sudden thought. It was, he reckoned, a true inspiration. In that moment he had figured out how he could solve the hitherto insoluble problem of Lizzie Reardon. He chuckled, then beckoned Little Billy who by now had appeared in the doorway of the ranch house.

'Li'l Billy,' Big John barked, 'pick up this here Injun an' carry him into the house.'

Little Billy stared at his father in amazement.

'You serious, Pa?' he enquired. 'You wanta take that stinkin' redskin indoors?'

'I do.'

'But—'

'Jest do as I say, Li'l Billy,' rasped Big John.

Little Billy noted the edge to his father's voice and made no further protest. Instead, he hurried over to where Naches lay, bent down and picked up the dead Apache. Then he carried him in his arms up on to the porch and into the ranch house. Big John followed and, once he had hitched his horse to the rail outside, he, too, entered the building.

By this time Larry and Danny Docherty had picked themselves up and they helped their younger brother lay out the young Apache's corpse in one corner of the kitchen.

'Why are we doin' this?' asked a puzzled Larry Docherty.

'I dunno,' replied Little Billy. 'It was Pa's idea that we bring him into the house.'

'But why, Pa?' demanded Danny.

' 'Cause he's gonna play a part in a scheme I've jest devised to save you three lunkheads from the gallows.'

'But he's dead, Pa!' exclaimed Little Billy.

'I know that.'

'Then how in blue blazes is he gonna help us? An', anyways, whaddya mean 'bout savin' us from the gallows?' rasped Larry.

' 'Course, you don't know,' said Big John.

'Know what?' asked Danny.

'That the gal who witnessed you shootin' those folks on the stagecoach ain't bound for El Paso. She's stayin' here in Burro Creek, where she's takin' up the post of schoolmistress.'

'Jeeze!'

'Yeah. So, unless you boys steer clear of town, sooner or later she's sure to spot you.'

'But won't it strike folks as strange if'n we suddenly stop callin' at the store an' the saloon? They're bound to start askin' questions,' said Larry.

'Yup.'

'An' if they should link our non-appearance with the hold-up. . . ?'

'Which is possible. There were three road-agents an' there are three of you. I'd planned to tell anyone who asked that you were busy roundin' up some hosses that had run off. 'Course, while that would have bought us a li'l time, it could only work as an excuse in the short term.' Big John smiled grimly and continued, 'Then I returned here jest in time to observe them Apaches runnin' off our hosses. An' I succeeded in shootin' one of the varmints. Which gave me an idea.'

'Waal, I cain't see how that dead Injun is gonna help us any,' declared Larry.

'Me neither,' said Danny.

'So, tell us what you've got in mind, Pa,' said Little Billy.

'Certainly. I ain't worked out every last detail, but the basic plan is this . . .' And Big John went on to explain to his sons what he had in mind.

When he had finished, there was a short silence while the three brothers mulled over their father's scheme.

'I reckon your plan might jest work!' exclaimed Larry enthusiastically.

'Me, too,' added Danny, while Little Billy nodded his agreement.

'OK. Waal, till this is all settled, I want you boys to lay off the whiskey,' said Big John sternly.

The brothers looked decidedly crestfallen.

'But, Pa—' began Larry.

'No buts. Two of you can spend what's left of the afternoon out searchin' for them hosses the Apaches ran off. I don't expect you'll find 'em, but you can try,' retorted Big John.

'Ain't you comin' with us?' asked Little Billy.

'Nope. I'm headin' back into Burro Creek. I need to discuss my scheme with Sidney Bailey. An', while

I'm in town. I'll let it be known that the ranch has been raided by a band of young Apaches an' that, in consequence, you boys are out tryin' to round up some of the hosses they took. An', let's hope that, by 'bout this time tomorrow, Miss Lizzie Reardon will no longer be a threat to us.'

'Miss Lizzie Reardon. So, that's the name of that gal who gave us the slip,' said Larry. 'Hmm. This time she ain't gonna be so lucky,' he growled menacingly.

'She sure ain't,' asserted his father.

'You said two of us should ride after them missin' hosses,' said Danny.

'I did. You an' Larry. Li'l Billy, meantime, will stay here an' guard that thar Injun's corpse 'gainst any attempt by the Apaches to retrieve it.'

'You think they'll try, Pa?' asked Little Billy.

'They may do, an' I ain't takin' no chances. We need that corpse.'

'OK, Pa.'

'We'll give it a coupla hours. If'n we ain't found them hosses by then, Danny an' me, we'll head back here an' keep Li'l Billy company,' said Larry.

'Right. Let's git goin'.'

So saying, Big John Docherty headed for the door. He was closely followed by Larry and Danny, while Little Billy went in search of a shotgun. He intended sitting outside on the porch and keeping a look-out for any sight of the Apaches. Firstly, however, he tied Naches's small black pony to the hitching-rail. At the same time Big John unhitched his chestnut mare and mounted her while Larry and Danny fetched their horses from the stables.

A few minutes later Little Billy had only the dead brave for company. Larry and Danny had ridden out on to the plain on what they anticipated being a fruitless search, and Big John Docherty was heading, for a second time that day, in the direction of Burro Creek.

Upon arriving in town Big John's first port of call was the law office, where he found Sheriff Lew Flood deep in conversation with Hiram C. Lancaster.

The sheriff looked up enquiringly and asked, 'What brings you to my office, Big John? I don't s'pose you've come to bring news 'bout them murderin' sonsofbitches who held up the stage?'

The big rancher shook his head.

'Nope,' he said. ''Fraid not. Was that what you an' the mayor was discussin'?'

'It was indeed. A dreadful business,' commented Lancaster.

'Yeah. Waal, I got some more bad news,' said Big John.

'Go on,' growled Flood.

'You know that bunch of young Apache bucks who've been indulgin' in their form of Springtime frolics, firin' off their rifles an' runnin' off folks' cattle an' hosses an' makin' a general nuisance of theirselves?'

'Yup.'

'They raided my ranch less than an hour back an' ran off a dozen or more of my hosses.'

'Holy cow, it never rains but it pours!' exclaimed the sheriff. 'The stage gits held up, all those folks git shot and then those goddam Injuns strike, all in the same day!'

'Doesn't seem the three deppities you sent out lookin' for the Apaches have had much luck,' said the mayor glumly.

'It sure don't, Hiram. I guess they're wastin' their time out there, wherever they are.' Flood turned and addressed the rancher. 'Jest as soon as they return, I'll send 'em out your way, Big John. See if they can pick up the Apaches' trail.'

'OK, Sheriff.' Big John did not sound particularly enthusiastic, for he had little or no confidence in their ability to do so. 'Meantime, I got my boys out lookin' for my missin' hosses,' he said.

'I wish 'em luck,' said Flood.

'Me, too,' added Lancaster.

'I'll leave you to it, then,' said Big John.

'Yeah. 'Bye, Big John.'

' 'Bye, Sheriff. 'Bye, Mr Mayor.'

As he crossed Main Street and headed towards the Burro Creek Hotel, Big John passed the young deputy, Frank McCoy, who was in the process of doing his rounds of the town. Frank smiled and tipped his Stetson.

' 'Afternoon, Mr Docherty,' he drawled.

Upon reaching the hotel, Big John hastened up the short flight of wooden steps to the stoop. Then he pushed open the front door of the hotel and entered. He made his way along a narrow lobby to where a thin, bald-headed clerk stood behind the reception desk.

'Mr Bailey in his office?' enquired Big John.

'Yessir,' replied the clerk.

'Fine.'

Big John turned, retreated a few steps and tapped on the door to his left. On receiving the command to enter, he stepped into Sidney Bailey's office. The young hotel manager was seated behind his desk, exactly as he had been on Big John's earlier visit.

'Goddammit, Big John, what the hell are you doin' back here?' exclaimed Bailey.

'We need to talk,' said the rancher, drawing up a chair and sitting down opposite him.

'Again?'

'Yeah, again.'

'Look, the less contact we have the better. Anyways, I thought we'd agreed to meet sometime tomorrow?'

'That's right.'

'So?'

'So, I've brought our meetin' forward. Y'see I've come up with a plan, which I b'lieve will solve our li'l problem.'

Sidney Bailey's eyes lit up. He had been mulling the matter over in his mind and had so far come up with nothing.

'Go on, Big John,' he said eagerly.

'After our last meetin' I headed back to the ranch an' arrived jest as that bunch of young Apache bucks who are currently rampagin' through the county chose to swoop in an' raid my spread. They drove off several of my stock of hosses, but I succeeded in shootin' down one of 'em.'

'Well done. But where does that git us?'

'It gave me an idea. A sudden inspiration, I s'pose you'd call it.'

'Oh, yeah?'

'Yeah.' Big John grinned broadly and went on, 'I figured if'n Miss Lizzie Reardon got herself shot by an Injun, that'd surely git us off the hook.'

Bailey stared nonplussed at the rancher.

' 'Course it would,' he said. 'But how in tarnation are you gonna persuade an Injun to shoot her? Hell, seems all you've got is a dead 'un!'

'Which is all I need,' said Big John.

'You're proposin' that a dead Injun should shoot Miss Reardon?' exclaimed Bailey in disbelief.

'Exactly.'

'You're crazy!'

Big John continued to grin broadly.

'No, I ain't,' he said. 'Let me explain.'

'Please do.'

'It's like this. I'm gonna need your participation in this here scheme of mine. After school tomorrow I want you to take Miss Reardon out for a ride in one of the hotel gigs. D'you think you can manage that?'

'I reckon so.'

By now Sidney Bailey was intrigued. He was no longer of the opinion that Big John had taken leave of his senses.

'Good!' Big John stared the other straight in the eye and rasped, 'A pleasant country ride is what's required, showin' our new schoolmistress the more picturesque parts of our county.'

'Where d'you have in mind?'

'There's Sandy Banks, a favourite spot for the town's children to play at. An' there's Two-Mile Hollow, further out on the plain an' set in the midst of cottonwoods, with that pretty li'l stream runnin' through it an' a fine view of the San Andres mountains. I suggest you take Miss Reardon first of all to Sandy Banks an' then on to Two-Mile Hollow, where my boys will be lyin' in wait. They'll have that dead Apache I spoke of strapped across the back of his pony an' I'll detail one of 'em to shoot Miss Reardon. Then all you've gotta do is ride into town with the two corpses an' explain that the Apache ambushed you.'

'An' that, in the resultin' gunfight, he shot Lizzie Reardon dead 'fore I could shoot him,' said Bailley, grinning. 'That's brilliant, Big John! Hell, it's foolproof!'

'Yeah. Waal, don't forgit to carry a rifle in the gig an' be sure to fire off at least one shot. Jest in case anyone decides to check your gun.'

'There's no reason why anyone should.'

'No, but let's take no chances. Some folks have suspicious natures.'

'OK.'

'You're happy with my plan an' the part you have to play in it?'

'Yeah, Big John, I sure am.'

'Then, I reckon you'd best call round an' issue that invitation to Miss Reardon.'

'Now?'

'Yup.'

'But it's less than a coupla hours since I was round Miss Peel's an' speakin' to her.'

'We cain't afford to delay. That dead Injun ain't gonna keep for too long. If'n we don't move quickly, his corpse is likely to deteriorate an' then we won't be able to fool nobody. You gotta persuade her to take that ride tomorrow afternoon.'

Bailey nodded. The need for swift action was undeniable. If only, he thought, Big John Docherty's sons had made certain that all who had ridden in the stagecoach were dead before they removed their masks. His plan, too, had seemed foolproof. But it hadn't been. Three fools had scuppered it. He prayed that those same three fools wouldn't scupper Big John's. Surely even Larry, Danny and Little Billy could be relied upon this time to get it right? At least, Bailey consoled himself, Big John wasn't expecting him to shoot Lizzie Reardon.

'I'll go straight away,' he said.

111

'An' I'll wait here for you to come back with Miss Reardon's answer. I jest hope an' pray it'll be the right one,' said Big John.

'Certainly, I'll do my darnedest to persuade her to take that ride,' promised Sidney Bailey, rising from behind his desk.

'You do that.'

Big John waited until Bailey had vacated the office, then went across and began opening the cupboards which lined one of its walls. It was in the second cupboard that he discovered the glass and the bottle of Bailey's best Bourbon. This fine old whiskey was kept exclusively for the hotelier's own consumption. Big John chuckled as he removed the cork and poured a generous measure into the glass.

Bailey, meantime, headed once more along Main Street towards Miss Violet Peel's one-storey red-brick house. He tapped gently on her front door, and a few moments later, it was opened by Violet. A look of surprise suffused the schoolmistress's face upon observing her caller.

'Oh, Mr Bailey!' she exclaimed. 'Back so soon!'

'Er . . . yes. I . . . er . . . I had not intended to call upon you again until later in the week, when I proposed to fix a time an' a date for that tea I spoke of.'

'Yes. And I am sure Miss Reardon and I are looking forward to it,' said Violet. 'But, if you have not come to speak about the tea, what, then, is the purpose of your visit?'

'It occurred to me that, following her first day at

school, Miss Reardon might be glad of a little fresh air. The thought came to me that a short ride round the county, takin' in its more picturesque aspects, would perhaps appeal to her an' at the same time give her an appetite for supper.'

'I am sure she will have that whether or not she accepts your offer of a ride. However, it is kind of you to think of her. So, please come in and ask her. We won't be eating until after six, so there is certainly sufficient time to enjoy a brief excursion.'

'Thank you. And I'll be sure to git her back in good time for her meal.'

Sidney Bailey removed his hat and stepped into the house. Violet closed the door behind him before leading him across a narrow hall to the small sitting room in which he had earlier that day spoken to the two ladies.

Here he found Lizzie Reardon and, after exchanging the usual civilities, he repeated what he had just told Violet, concluding, 'It would be my pleasure to show you the county at its best. There are several beautiful spots where, in the future, you may care to picnic.'

'That is true,' added Violet. 'I am sure you would enjoy the ride, my dear.'

Lizzie was not quite so certain. While Sidney Bailey was not handsome, neither was he ugly. He was, she supposed, rather ordinary-looking, and he seemed to be a kind young man. Yet some instinct deep inside her caused her to hesitate. There was something about him. . . .

'I . . . I don't ride,' she stammered.

Bailey smiled.

'Oh, I don't expect you to ride a horse!' he said reassuringly. 'I have me a rather comfortable li'l gig. We'll ride in that.'

'There you are, my dear!' said Violet.

'Well . . . er . . . it's very kind of you,' replied Lizzie, uncertainly.

'Not at all. It's what you need after all you've been through: a quiet, restful circuit of the local beauty spots.'

'Mr Bailey is quite right. The ride will do you good,' reiterated Violet. 'And Mr Bailey has promised to get you home in good time for supper,' she added by way of encouragement.

'Indeed I have. So, what do you say, Miss Reardon?' he asked anxiously.

Lizzie felt that she could scarcely refuse. And why should she? she asked herself. To do so would be churlish and only because of some totally irrational antipathy she felt towards him.

'Thank you, Mr Bailey. I should be delighted to accept your kind offer,' lied Lizzie, while at the same time she forced a smile.

'Splendid!' said Violet. She did not have to force her smile.

Neither did Bailey. Part one of Big John Docherty's murderous plan had been accomplished. Now it remained to be seen whether part two would be equally successful.

'At what time does school finish for the day?' he asked.

'Three-thirty,' said Violet.

'I shall be there waiting for you,' Bailey informed Lizzie. 'Until tomorrow afternoon, then.'

'Yes. Until tomorrow afternoon,' repeated Lizzie.

She remained in the sitting room while Violet escorted their visitor to the door. There he took his leave of the schoolmistress and headed back to the hotel.

By the time Bailey returned to his office, Big John had consumed a third of a bottle of his best Bourbon. Bailey stretched across the desk, snatched up the rancher's half-empty glass and hastily gulped back the remains of the whiskey.

Big John eyed the young hotelier with some anxiety.

'Waal?' he growled. 'How'd it go?'

Sidney Bailey grinned and slammed the glass back down on to the desk.

'It's settled. Me an' Miss Lizzie Reardon set off at three-thirty tomorrow afternoon for a nice, leisurely drive round the county,' he stated.

'Endin' up at Two-Mile Hollow?'

'Of course.'

'The boys'll be there waitin' for you.'

So saying, Big John rose from behind the desk and made for the door.

'You ain't gonna be there?' enquired Bailey.

'Nope. The boys landed us in this mess. I reckon on leavin' it to them to put matters right,' declared the rancher.

Thereupon he left the hotel and headed for the Hot Spurs Saloon, where he intended enjoying a couple of beers and spreading the word that Chaco and his band had raided the horse ranch. He would repeat what he had told the sheriff and the mayor, that the Apaches had driven off several of his horses and that his three sons were out looking for them. This would, he figured, satisfactorily explain their non-appearance in the saloon that evening.

As a consequence of his visit to the Hot Spurs, Big John arrived back at the ranch only a few minutes before Larry and Danny hove into sight, driving a small herd of horses before them. Much to their surprise they had found the horses abandoned by the Apaches and had had little trouble in bringing them home.

Once all three were reunited in the ranch house with Little Billy, Big John explained what had taken place in Burro Creek.

'An' so,' he concluded, 'by this time tomorrow, all our troubles should be over. Jest make sure there ain't no mistake. I want Miss Lizzie Reardon good'n dead!'

'Don't worry. Pa. I'll personally take care of the gal. With this,' said Larry, slapping the butt of his Winchester.

They all laughed.

'Does this call for a drink?' asked Danny hope-fully.

Big John scowled and shook his head.

'Nope. We got that dead Injun to take care of,' he rasped.

'Aw, but Pa! Them Apaches ain't gonna come lookin' for him!' protested Danny.

'We don't know that for certain. An' we ain't takin' no chances. We'll split the night into watches, two hours at a time. Me an' Li'l Billy will take the first stretch, so you can git your heads down,' Big John informed the two older brothers.

There were no more protests. And so the vigil began.

Meanwhile, outside in the darkness and no further than fifty yards from the ranch house lurked Chaco, the Apache band's young leader.

When the Apaches had regrouped under the lee of a hill a couple of miles from the Dochertys' ranch, they had discovered that Naches was missing. None had noticed his absence during their flight, so intent had they been on driving the stolen horses before them. Now they abandoned the horses while they discussed what might have happened to him.

One or two suggested that they all return to the ranch, for it seemed certain that Naches must be there, perhaps taken prisoner? Chaco firmly vetoed this proposal. What up until then had been a highly successful series of raids had suddenly ended in disaster. Chaco was convinced that Naches was either dead or held by the white men. An attack upon the ranch would determine which, but this might at the same time result in the deaths of several other braves. Chaco could not risk that. He was their leader. It was he whom his uncle, the chief of the Chiricahua Apaches, would hold responsible. Consequently he decided that he alone would return to the ranch.

So Chaco explained his plan to the others. He would make his way back to the ranch by a circuitous route, approaching it stealthily so that the white men would not spot him. He would then attempt to discover what had become of Naches and, if he were held prisoner, try to release him. Afterwards, he would meet up with the band at Eagle Rock, a rather desolate place in the foothills of the San Andres mountains, but no more than five or six miles from the ranch. In the event of his failing to arrive within the next twenty-four hours, he ordered them to go back to the Apache reservation and explain matters to their chief.

Chaco had then parted from the others, headed towards the ranch and, having left his pony hidden in a stand of cottonwoods, crawled the final couple of hundred yards to the nearest of Big John Docherty's outbuildings. He had immediately spotted Naches's horse tied to the rail outside the ranch house and commenced a thorough, yet cautious, search of all the ranch's barns and stables, but without success.

Later he had observed, firstly, the return of Big John, then Larry and Danny driving the recently released horses back to the ranch. What had they done with Naches? he wondered. Were they holding the young brave a prisoner inside the ranch house and, if so, for what purpose? He discounted the possibility that Naches had been taken into town since his pony stood in front of the ranch house.

Chaco settled down in the long prairie grass where, even during the daylight hours, he would remain hidden from view. It was his intention to watch and wait and, when eventually the white men made their move, act accordingly.

EIGHT

Frank McCoy's chance encounter that afternoon with Big John Docherty gave him pause for thought. What reason, he wondered, did the rancher have for visiting the Burro Creek Hotel? To his knowledge, Big John had never before entered the hotel. When visiting Burro Creek he had hitherto restricted his visits pretty much to the general store and the Hot Spurs Saloon. He had made an occasional visit to the blacksmith's forge, the feed-and-grain store and the barbering parlour, but not to the late Edward Tindall's establishment.

The young deputy decided to interrupt his rounds of the town for a few minutes while he kept surveillance on the hotel. He could have given no rational explanation as to why he had determined to do this. It was simply some instinct deep within him that prompted Frank to act as he did.

He proceeded to patrol up and down the sidewalk on the opposite side of Main Street to the hotel. He would saunter fifty yards in one direction, then return. It was during the course of his fourth perambulation that Frank McCoy spotted Sidney Bailey step out of the hotel and set off down Main Street. Frank promptly halted, turned round and, at a safe distance, followed the hotelier. His curiosity increased when he observed Bailey enter Violet Peel's house. What in tarnation was going on? he asked himself.

Frank and Stone had witnessed Bailey's earlier call. He had been in the act of leaving the house when they returned from their ride out to the spot where the stagecoach had been held up. Now the hotelier was paying a second visit. From where he stood the deputy could keep a watchful eye on both the Burro Creek Hotel and Miss Violet Peel's house.

Frank McCoy did not like to admit, even to himself, that it was more than just curiosity that caused him to continue with this surveillance. Had Bailey entered either the bank or the saloon, Frank would, in all probability, have resumed his circuit of the town. But he had not. And Frank suspected that it was Lizzie Reardon, rather than Violet Peel, upon whom Bailey was calling.

At twenty-two the deputy was sorely smitten. From the moment he had first set eyes on Lizzie, pale but beautiful, sitting up beside the Kentuckian on that stagecoach with its gruesome cargo of six corpses, he had fallen deeply in love with her. Now he feared that Sidney Bailey had stolen a march on him. Yet he still regarded it strange that Bailey should have made the second call so soon after the first. For what purpose, he wondered, and did Big John Docherty's visit to the hotel have anything to do with it? Of course, he told himself, he was assuming rather a lot; the rancher might not even have seen Bailey while in the hotel. Perhaps it was someone else whom Big John went to visit there?

Here Frank McCoy's thoughts were disrupted by the sudden reappearance of Sidney Bailey. Frank slipped off the sidewalk and into the shadows of a narrow alley, from where he could safely watch the hotelier retrace his steps and eventually vanish through the front door of his hotel. The deputy remained where he was for some further minutes and was rewarded by the sight of Big John Docherty emerging from the hotel, crossing the street and entering the Hot Spurs Saloon.

Frank continued to linger in the alley while he tried to make sense of what he had just witnessed. Various thoughts flitted through his mind and then, suddenly, he came up with an explanation. It was, however, an explanation that filled him with foreboding. If he was right in his conjecture, action was required.

He immediately headed for the law office, where he found Sheriff Lew Flood and Jack Stone sitting smoking cheroots and discussing the events of the day. The sheriff's eyes lit up as Frank McCoy stepped across the threshold.

'Ah, Frank!' he exclaimed. 'The very man. Jack an' me, we was aimin' to have us a few beers at the Hot Spurs. So, if you could mind the office for an hour or so?'

'Yeah, of course, Sheriff. But, 'fore you go, I got somethin' I wanta discuss with you,' said the young-ster.

'Sure, Frank; we ain't in no tearin' hurry, are we, Jack?' asked Flood.

'No, Lew, we ain't,' said the Kentuckian.

'So, Frank, fire ahead. What d'you need to discuss with me?'

'Waal, it's like this. I've been givin' the matter some thought an' I couldn't understand why them desperadoes who held up the stage had to kill all those folk. It didn't make no sense.'

'I've been thinkin' exactly the same, but mebbe there weren't no rhyme nor reason to it. P'rhaps the murderin' bastards shot 'em down for the sheer hell of it?'

'I don't think so.'

'No?'

'No, Sheriff. Some comin's an' goin's that I chanced to observe in the last half-hour have made me think otherwise. Let me explain.'

'I'm listenin', Frank.'

'Me, too,' added Stone, his pale blue eyes alight with curiosity.

'Firstly, you will recall, Mr Stone, that on our return from visitin' the scene of the hold-up, we saw

Sidney Bailey leavin' Miss Violet Peel's house.'

'Yup.'

'He was surely simply callin' to enquire after Miss Reardon followin' her terrible ordeal? I'd say that was perfectly natural,' remarked Flood.

'Mebbe, But I don't reckon the comin's an' goin's I've observed since then are so easily explained. One: 'bout half an hour ago Big John Docherty paid a visit to the Burro Creek Hotel. Not an everyday occurrence. 'Deed, Sheriff, can you ever remember seein' him enter that hotel?'

Flood frowned.

'Nope. I cain't say I have,' he admitted.

'Nor me.' Frank smiled grimly and went on, 'A few minutes later Sidney Bailey left the hotel an' proceeded along Main Street as far as Miss Peel's house, where he promptly made a second visit. Kinda soon after his first, wouldn't you say?'

'I s'pose.'

'Then, a while later, he returned to the hotel an', a few minutes after that, Big John Docherty emerged an' made his way to the Hot Spurs.'

'Where he doubtless informed all'n sundry 'bout the Apaches' raid on his hoss ranch,' said the sheriff.

'Jeeze, when did that happen?' asked his deputy in surprise.

'An hour or so back.'

'Wow! What a day! First the stage is held up an' all them folks is murdered, an' then those pesky Apache braves raid Big John's ranch.'

'That's right, Frank. I cain't remember a day like it,' said Flood. 'But, 'bout those comin's an' goin's you mentioned, how an' why d'you reckon they relate to the murder of Ed Tindall an' the others?'

'It . . . it's jest a theory,' replied Frank diffidently.

'Waal, out with it.'

When the idea had struck him, Frank had been convinced that he was right in his deduction. Now, in the presence of the sheriff and the Kentuckian, he was not quite so sure. Nevertheless, the youngster determined to expound his theory and see what his elders thought of it.

'Miss Reardon witnessed the hold-up an' saw the faces of the three road agents. Right?'

'Right, Frank.'

'So, whoever committed those murders would want her dead.'

'Agreed.'

'There were three of 'em.'

'Yeah You've already mentioned that.'

'An' Big John Docherty has three sons.'

'Hey, wait a minute, Frank! Are you suggestin' that them Docherty boys are the killers?'

'That's exactly what I'm suggestin'.'

'I know they ain't no angels. 'Deed, they've been involved in many a bar-room brawl. But cold-blooded murder is somethin' else altogether. Why would they kill all those folk?'

'For money. But not for what they took off their victims.'

'No?'

'No. My theory is that Sidney Bailey paid them. He's Mr Tindall's nephew an' was his heir. Then, a coupla weeks back, Mr Tindall got hisself engaged to Mrs Emma Younger. If'n they had gotten married, Sidney Bailey would no longer have been the heir.'

'But Ed Tindall wouldn't have cut him out completely. He'd have made some provision after all the years Bailey had worked for him.'

'Mebbe. Mebbe not. Anyways, Bailey would no longer have enjoyed the prospect of becomin' Burro Creek's richest citizen.'

'An' you figure he wanted that badly enough to contemplate murder?'

'I do, Sheriff.'

'But, even so, Big John Docherty—'

'Is, accordin' to rumour, almost broke. He an' his boys might jest have been desperate enough to do Sidney Bailey's biddin'. For the right price. Bailey would've known that his uncle was gonna be on that stage an', by gittin' the Docherty boys to kill all on board, he surely reckoned to make it seem Mr Tindall was merely one of several victims an' *not* the prime target.' Frank paused for breath and then continued, 'All these recent comin's an' goin's are what put the idea into my head.'

'Explain.'

'If I'm right, Big John Docherty's gotta be worried that, sooner or later, Miss Reardon is gonna spot one or other of his boys an' recognize him as one of the road agents. Hell, they cain't avoid comin' into town for evermore! So, I reckon Big John's formulated some plan to dispose of Miss Reardon 'fore that happens. Hence all the to-in' an' fro-in' between the hotel an' Miss Peel's house.'

'Oh, yeah?'

'Yes. My guess is that Big John needs Bailey's help an' Bailey sure ain't in no position to refuse. Therefore, Big John enters the hotel an' sends Bailey to pay a second call on Miss Reardon. Then, when Bailey has made that call, he reports back to Big John who then promptly leaves the hotel. The question is: what exactly is Big John's plan?'

'If there is such a plan,' growled Flood.

'It all adds up,' declared his deputy.

'In your head. But it's pure conjecture. What do you think, Jack?' Flood asked the Kentuckian.

Stone rubbed his jaw thoughtfully.

'You're sayin', Frank, that Mr Docherty sent Sidney Bailey round to visit Miss Reardon as part of his plan for her disposal,' he drawled.

'Yup. That's my theory, Mr Stone,' replied Frank firmly. The young man's diffidence had dissipated. Explaining his suspicions to the others had strengthened his belief that Big John and Sidney Bailey were indeed aiming to silence Lizzie Reardon. 'We gotta do somethin',' he pleaded.

'Hmm,' said Stone. Then, after some thought, he added, 'I agree.'

'But, Jack, this is, as I said, pure conjecture on

Frank's part,' protested the sheriff.

'Again I agree,' said Stone. 'However, jest suppose he's right. It does all hang together.'

'Mebbe.'

'We cain't afford to do nuthin', Sheriff!' cried Frank.

Lew Flood frowned as he ran over in his mind what his deputy had told him.

'No,' he conceded finally.

'So, what do we do?' demanded the youngster.

'I reckon we must follow Mr Bailey's example an' pay a call upon Miss Reardon,' said Stone.

'But we certainly cain't voice our suspicions to her,' stated the sheriff. 'There is such a thing as slander an', remember, we're law officers. If we wanta keep our jobs—'

'To hell with our jobs! If Miss Reardon's life is at stake—'

'If. That's the point, Frank; we don't know for sure.'

'Lew's right. We don't,' said Stone.

'So?'

'So, let's jest play this close to our chests,' suggested the Kentuckian.

'Whaddya mean?'

'I mean, we pay that visit. But we do as the sheriff says an' do *not* voice our suspicions. We simply claim, as I've no doubt Sidney Bailey did, that we are callin' to see how Miss Reardon is bearin' up after her terrible ordeal.' Stone smiled and added, ''An', at the same time, we try to find out what passed between her an' Bailey when he made that second visit.'

Frank grinned.

'OK, let's go,' he cried eagerly.

'Hold your hosses,'rasped Flood. 'It don't require all three of us to pay this here call.'

'Quite right, Lew. Whaddya suggest?' enquired Stone.

'I'll stay here an' mind the office. You an' Frank go. But bear in mind what I said: keep your suspicions to yourselves.'

'Sure thing, Lew.'

'OK, Frank?' Flood eyed his deputy anxiously.

'Yeah. I ... I agree,' confirmed the youngster, albeit somewhat reluctantly.

So it was settled. A few minutes later Jack Stone and Frank McCoy presented themselves at Violet Peel's front door.

The elderly schoolmistress opened the door and glanced up at the two men. She was clearly surprised.

'My! My!' she exclaimed. 'This is quite a day for gentlemen callers. I don't remember when I last received so many.'

'If it ain't convenient—' began the Kentuckian.

'No, do come in,' said Violet, though adding, 'I expect it's Miss Reardon you've come to see. So, if you'll forgive me, I'll retire to the kitchen. I'm in the midst of preparing supper, you see.'

'We could call later,' said Stone.

'No! No! It'll be half an hour yet before supper's ready and I don't suppose you'll be staying that long?'

'No, ma'am. We've jest called to ask after Miss Reardon. We'll be fairly brief.'

'Excellent.' Violet turned and led the two men through to the small sitting room where she and Lizzie had entertained Sidney Bailey. 'Two gentlemen to see you, my dear,' she informed an equally surprised Lizzie Reardon before disappearing into the kitchen.

'Why, Deputy McCoy and Mr Stone!' cried Lizzie.

'We thought we'd call to see how you were bearin' up,' explained Stone.

'That's very kind of you,' acknowledged Lizzie.

'Not at all. We . . . we are anxious that you should think well of Burro Creek. It is really a very nice place to live an' we both hope you'll be very happy here,' declared Frank McCoy, blushing as he spoke.

'I'm sure I shall be,' said Lizzie, bestowing upon him a warm smile, which caused him to blush even more.

'What you experienced out on the trail ain't somethin' we're used to in these parts,' continued Frank. 'It's usually pretty peaceful round here. Sometimes there's a li'l cattle-rustlin' out on the plains, but that's about all.'

'Yeah, I guess you was real unlucky to git caught up in that thar hold-up,' commented Stone.

'But lucky to survive it,' said the girl feelingly.

'Yes, Miss Reardon, that you were,' he agreed.

'I don't suppose those murderers have been caught?' she murmured.

Frank McCoy shook his head.

'No,' he said sadly and then, to reassure the girl, he added, tongue in cheek, 'I expect they're many miles away by now.'

'Yes.'

'Miss Peel indicated that we ain't the only persons to call today an' wish you well,' said Stone.

'No. Mr Tindall's nephew called,' said Lizzie. Tears formed in her eyes as she remarked, 'Mr Tindall was such a nice, kind man, a proper gentleman.'

'He was,' agreed Frank. 'He'll be much missed.'

'I s'pose Mr Bailey also wanted to enquire how you were doin' after your ordeal?' said Stone.

'Yes. He called twice as a matter of fact,' said Lizzie.

'Indeed?'

'Yes, Mr Stone. On the second occasion, he called to ask me if I would care to accompany him on a short ride round the county, to view its beauty spots.'

'You ride, Miss Reardon?'

'No. Mr Bailey proposes to take me in a gig.'

'An' have you accepted Mr Bailey's offer?' asked Frank anxiously.

'I have. It would have been churlish to refuse.'

' 'Course,' said Stone. 'An' jest when does this li'l excursion take place?'

'Tomorrow afternoon. Mr Bailey is to pick me up outside the schoolhouse at half past three when school breaks up.'

'Waal, I hope you have a pleasant ride,' said Stone.

'Me, too,' added Frank McCoy, although, in truth, he did no such thing. He certainly had no wish that Lizzie should enjoy Sidney Bailey's company.

'Guess we'd best be on our way, then,' said Stone. 'Miss Peel said she was preparin' supper an', 'sides, we got business to attend to.'

'Well, thank you for calling. It was very kind of you to enquire after me,' said Lizzie.

'Our pleasure,' said the Kentuckian.

'Er . . . yes . . . our pleasure,' stammered the young deputy, colouring once again.

Lizzie escorted them to the front door, while from the kitchen there emanated the sounds and smells of Violet Peel's cooking.

On the walk back to the law office Frank McCoy's mind was buzzing. The short visit had only served to increase and deepen his feelings towards Lizzie Reardon. But what chance did he have of securing her affections? Precious little, he thought bitterly, for how could he compete with Sidney Bailey, soon to become the richest man in town, if not in the entire county? Then he recalled Lizzie's response to his question regarding Bailey's offer of a ride. She had simply said that it would be churlish to refuse. Not exactly the reply he would have expected from someone overjoyed at the prospect. The young man's heart leapt. Could it be that Lizzie had no real inclination to ride out with Bailey? And then, he suddenly recalled, there were his suspicions regarding Bailey's true intentions towards the girl. But he had no opportunity to pursue these thoughts any further, for by now they had reached, and were about to enter, the law office.

Sheriff Lew Flood looked up from behind his desk as his deputy and the Kentuckian pushed open the door and stepped into the office. A look of expectancy adorned the peace officer's usually impassive face.

'Waal,' he demanded, 'how'd it go? What, if anythin', did you find out?'

'It was like this,' replied Stone and he went on to relate everything that had passed during the course of his and Frank McCoy's visit.

'So, where does this git us?' growled Flood.

'I dunno,' said Stone. 'We know that Sidney Bailey an' Miss Reardon plan a short ride round the more picturesque parts of the county.'

'A plan that is in all likelihood perfectly innocent,' remarked the sheriff.

'Mebbe.'

'Or mebbe not,' interjected Frank. 'It could have been concocted during the course of those meetin's at the Burro Creek Hotel 'tween Bailey an' Big John Docherty.'

'If the two met there. We don't know for sure that

133

it was Bailey Big John went to see,' commented the sheriff.

'No, but I'll bet it was.'

'I agree,' said Stone.

'Waal, assumin' you're both right, what d'you reckon they have in mind?' asked Flood.

'If I'm also right 'bout the Docherty boys bein' the men who held up the stage, then they are gonna want Miss Reardon dead,' stated Frank.

'So, Sidney Bailey takes her out for a ride, startin' from the schoolhouse. Hell, Miss Peel an' all the schoolchildren will witness them ridin' off together! He ain't gonna try nuthin'. How can he?'

'I'm not sure.'

'Jack, whaddya think?'

'Like Frank, I'm not sure what he has in mind. But I reckon he's up to somethin' an', whatever it is, it's gonna happen on that ride.'

'OK.' Flood frowned. 'So, what do we do? I s'pose there's only one thing we can do. We gotta trail 'em when they set out tomorrow, but at a discreet distance. They must on no account realize that they're bein' followed,' he said.

Frank McCoy's heart leapt a second time.

'I'll trail 'em, Sheriff,' he volunteered eagerly.

Lew Flood smiled at his young deputy.

'Sure, Frank,' he said, adding, 'I'd like to join you, but with the others still out searchin' for that young buck, Chaco, an' his band of Chiricahua Apaches, I guess I'll need to remain here in town.'

'I'll ride along with Frank if'n that's OK,' drawled Stone.

'I'd 'preciate that, Jack,' replied the sheriff.

'Me, too, Mr Stone,' said Frank.

'Then that's settled. We jest gotta wait an' see what tomorrow brings,' said the Kentuckian.

'But now how's 'bout them few beers we was aimin' to have?' Flood turned to the young deputy. 'You still happy to hold the fort?' he asked.

'Yeah, Sheriff. I'll remain here an' keep an eye on things,' said Frank.

'Good man! C'mon, Jack, I got me one helluva thirst,' declared Flood.

So saying, he and the Kentuckian vacated the law office and headed off towards the Hot Spurs Saloon. Frank McCoy, meantime, made himself comfortable behind the sheriff's large mahogany desk.

NINE

The following afternoon found Jack Stone and Deputy Frank McCoy at the window of the law office, closely observing the street outside. Stone had earlier spotted Sidney Bailey drive a gig out of the livery stables and round to the front of the Burro Creek Hotel. Now they were waiting for him to drive past on his way to the schoolhouse, which stood at the far end of Main Street.

Shortly before half past three their vigil was rewarded. As Bailey drove past Stone turned and informed the sheriff, who was busily engaged in some paperwork, 'OK, Lew, our quarry has jest ridden by.'

Lew Flood looked up from his labours.

'Good luck,' he said. 'An' be careful not to let him become aware you're trailin' him.'

'Don't worry, I've done this kinda thing before,' drawled the Kentuckian.

'Sure you have, Jack. An' I pray that you an' Frank

will bring this entire sorry business to a successful conclusion. Assumin', of course, that we are right in our premise.'

'We're right,' declared Frank McCoy confidently.

Then, without more ado, the young deputy and the big Kentuckian left the law office and proceeded to unhitch their horses from the rail outside.

By the time they had mounted, Sidney Bailey and his gig had reached the far end of Main Street. They watched as he turned to his left and vanished from sight.

'Jeeze, Mr Stone, let's git after him! We don't wanta lose him!' cried Frank.

Stone grinned.

'Take it easy, young feller,' he said. 'School ain't out yet awhile.'

'Sorry. Guess I'm a mite anxious,' confessed Frank.

'That's OK. It's only natural you should be. But bear in mind what the sheriff said: We mustn't let Bailey realize we're on his trail.'

'No, 'course not.' Frank smiled wryly. 'I'll take my cue from you, Mr Stone,' he promised.

They trotted slowly down Main Street and halted outside the late Edward Tindall's feed-and-grain store. Beyond that establishment the trail wound its way out across the plain, northwards towards Mesilla.

Jack Stone quickly dismounted.

'Stay where you are, Frank,' he instructed the deputy.

Then the Kentuckian slowly, cautiously, approached the far end of the building. He flattened himself against it and peered round the corner. As he did so the sound of a bell ringing shattered the silence, immediately followed by the excited cries of the children as they were released from school. Stone remained where he was and watched events. He observed the two schoolmistresses leave the school, Miss Peel pause to lock up and then bid farewell to her young colleague, whom, in the meantime, Sidney Bailey had helped into the gig.

Stone promptly retraced his steps and mounted his bay gelding. He turned to Frank McCoy.

'They're 'bout to set off,' he whispered. 'So, let's make ourselves scarce.'

Straight away he turned the gelding's head and trotted back up Main Street about fifty yards, to where it was crossed by East Street. He altered course into East Street, closely followed by Frank. Then he turned round and once more dismounted. From the corner of the street he was able to observe the gig's progress. Once it had disappeared round the first bend in the trail he again retraced his steps and mounted the gelding.

'Let's go!' he cried.

'Yessir!' responded Frank enthusiastically.

They proceeded along the trail at a reasonably fast trot. Each time they spotted the gig ahead of them they slackened their pace until it vanished round the next of the many bends in the Butterfield stage route. In this manner the two pursuers continued in the wake of Sidney Bailey's gig and witnessed it turning off down the fork which led to the picturesque spot known as Sandy Banks. They immediately rode their horses into the small stand of cottonwoods that stood upon the northern side of the fork. From here they could safely keep watch on the gig and its occupants. Nothing of any note happened. Bailey and his lovely young companion simply climbed out of the gig, stood for a few minutes admiring the view, and then climbed back into it. Thereupon, Bailey turned it round and headed back towards the main trail. Jack Stone and Frank McCoy swiftly backed their horses deeper into the wood, where they remained until the gig passed by.

The pursuit continued and, a mile or so further along the trail, the gig again turned off. This time it headed down a fork on the opposite, western side of the stage route.

'Where does that lead to?' Stone enquired of the deputy.

'Another well-known local beauty spot. It's known as Two-Mile Hollow,' replied Frank.

'Because it's two miles from Burro Creek?'

'Yup. It lies almost due west of the town. The trail we're now followin' will soon wind its way southward towards that short range of low hills.' Frank pointed to the hills off to their left, sprouting up out of the plain. 'For the moment, we continue westward,' he said.

Jack Stone nodded and urged his horse forward. He and the young deputy resumed their pursuit, again holding back whenever they spied the gig and proceeding only when it had disappeared round the next bend. Thus, they slowly approached the hills, the lower slopes of which were covered in a mixture of trees and scrub.

Ahead of them Sidney Bailey's gig rattled along the trail, with both the hotelier and his fair companion completely unaware that they were being pursued.

Lizzie Reardon had begun to relax and chide herself for having entertained doubts about Bailey. He, for his part, had proved to be a charming companion, reasonably attentive and keen to point out anything that he felt might prove of interest to her. The ride in the fresh air and taking in the most picturesque aspects of Dawson County had, as Violet Peel had forecast, proved most enjoyable. Sandy Banks, for instance, was certainly a spot where, sometime in the future, Lizzie would like to picnic.

Two-Mile Hollow lay on the very edge of the foothills. It was tree-lined and consisted of a small, flower-bedecked meadow with a stream running through it. As the gig drew to a halt in its centre, Lizzie concluded that this tranquil, verdant arbour would also be an ideal place for a picnic.

This happy thought was suddenly vanquished,

however, for scarcely had they halted when three horsemen rode out from amongst the trees and confronted them. Although clad in their usual workaday clothes, rather than the long brown leather coats and grey Stetsons that they had been wearing when they held up the stagecoach, the Docherty brothers were immediately recognized by Lizzie.

She paled instantly, gasped and cried out, 'Mr Bailey, get us out of here! Quickly! Those men are the ones who murdered your uncle and the others!'

Sidney Bailey smiled contemptuously.

'Of course they are,' he sneered. 'Do you seriously think that their appearance here is a coincidence?'

'What! What do you mean?' demanded Lizzie. 'What are you saying?'

'I'm sayin', Miss Reardon, that you gotta die. It's regrettable, but necessary, I'm afraid.'

'You . . . you brought me here with this in mind?'

'Yup.'

'But . . . but why?'

'Because you're the only person who could identify them as the men who held up that stage.'

'What on earth has that to do with you? Why should you care?'

' 'Cause Mr Bailey an' us, we're in cahoots,' Larry Docherty interjected.

'Yeah,' added Little Billy. 'It was on account of him that we held up the stage an' shot all them folk.'

'I don't understand.'

'His uncle, Ed Tindall, was Burro Creek's richest

citizen an' was set to leave everythin' to Mr Bailey when he died. Only recently Ed Tindall became engaged to a widder woman named Emma Younger, a young widder,' explained Danny.

'That's right,' said Larry.

Lizzie turned to face Sidney Bailey. Her features were ashen, her eyes wide with fear.

'I couldn't let that happen,' said Bailey. 'I'd worked long'n hard for a whole decade in the expectation of one day succeedin' Uncle Ed as Burro Creek's richest citizen. I wasn't prepared to let no widder woman stand in my way. A young widder, she might well have had children an' where would that leave me? I knew Uncle Ed was returnin' to Burro Creek on that thar stage an', so, I arranged for these boys to hold it up an' shoot all on board. That way nobody would have reason to suspect me of havin' any hand in my uncle's death.'

'You . . . you're a monster!' cried Lizzie.

Bailey laughed harshly.

'Call me what you will,' he said. 'It don't matter. But, believe me, I'm real sorry that you have to die. It's jest that me an' the boys, we couldn't risk you runnin' across them in town. Sooner or later, you'd've been sure to meet.'

'They could've stayed out of town,' replied Lizzie quietly.

'Not indefinitely.'

Lizzie choked back a sob and, as she did so, she suddenly noticed the small black pony which Little

Billy was trailing behind him. It was a moment or two before she realized that the object strapped across the pony's back was in fact a corpse. She pointed towards it.

'What's that?' she gasped. 'Is it. . . ?'

'An Injun. A dead Injun,' rasped Larry. He stared at Sidney Bailey and said, 'Let's git this over with.'

'Are you the one who…?' began Bailey.

'I am.'

Larry Docherty reached back and hefted the Winchester out of his saddleboot. He raised the rifle to his shoulder and took aim.

As he did so, Lizzie turned and, before Bailey could grab her, leapt from the gig. Larry swivelled round in the saddle and adjusted his aim. The girl had stumbled as she landed and, upon rising to her feet, presented Larry with the perfect target. He smiled wickedly, his finger on the trigger.

The gunshot rang out across the hollow and echoed throughout the nearby hills. Larry Docherty's Winchester slipped from his grasp and he fell forward out of the saddle, to land with a thump on the turf beneath. A few yards behind him, the young Apache, Chaco, had emerged from the trees. He, too, carried a Winchester and it was his bullet that had struck Larry in the back of the skull and blasted his brains out.

Danny and Little Billy wheeled their horses round, at the same time stretching back to grab hold of their rifles. But they were too late. Screeching a

143

wild, triumphant war cry, Chaco galloped towards them, firing as he came. His second shot struck Danny between the eyes and his third thumped into Little Billy's chest and knocked him clean out of the saddle.

Little Billy was down, but not out. He staggered to his feet, blood streaming from the wound in his chest. He turned to face the fast-approaching Indian. Since he had dropped his rifle, Little Billy now hastily pulled the Colt Peacemaker from its holster. But before he could raise it and take aim Chaco was upon him. The Apache had reversed the Winchester and was clutching it by the barrel. He swung it with all the fury he could muster. The wooden butt smashed into Little Billy's face with incredible force, smashing his nose and teeth. He cried out and fell to the ground, whereupon Chaco leapt from his pony and proceeded to hammer his skull with one ferocious blow after another until he was satisfied that Little Billy was well and truly dead.

From his position in the gig Sidney Bailey watched, horror-stricken, as the Apache killed the Docherty brothers one after the other. Then he turned the gig about and made to set off in pursuit of Lizzie, who was by now fleeing from the scene. As he did so, Jack Stone and Frank McCoy came galloping round the last bend in the trail before the hollow. Both men had drawn their revolvers and, viewing the carnage, straight away aimed their guns at Chaco as he stood astride Little Billy's blood-soaked corpse.

'No!' cried Lizzie. 'No! Don't shoot the Indian! He has just saved my life!'

The girl's words caused the pair to reassess the picture in front of them. They swiftly averted their aim from the young Apache and, as they drew abreast of the girl, Frank leapt from the saddle and gathered her up into his arms. Stone, meanwhile, reined in his gelding and aimed his Frontier Model Colt at the hotelier.

'Pull up an' stick your hands in the air!' he yelled.

Bailey reluctantly did as he was bid, his face full of apprehension. He desperately wanted to flee the scene, but realized that he had no chance of escaping. He climbed down from the gig. Stone dismounted and promptly stepped up to Bailey and began to search him. He found a derringer hidden up the hotelier's sleeve and confiscated it. As he did so, Frank McCoy and Lizzie Reardon approached. The deputy's arm enveloped the girl's shoulders and she leant gratefully against him.

'You ... you mustn't believe everything Miss Reardon says. All this shootin' an' killin' has likely confused her,' said Bailey in one last despairing attempt to exonerate himself.

'Shuddup!'

Stone gruffly uttered the single-word command and then immediately transferred his gaze to the Apache still standing above Little Billy's battered corpse.

Chaco stared defiantly back at the Kentuckian. He had adjusted his grip on the Winchester and now held it by the butt. The barrel pointed at the ground halfway between himself and Stone.

'As I said, I owe him my life, Mr Stone,' declared Lizzie, pointing at the Indian.

'Is that right?' growled Stone, while retaining his hold on Sidney Bailey, his Frontier Model Colt pressed hard into the hotelier's ribs.

'Yes. Yes. These men he has killed are the ones who held up the stagecoach. They were going to murder me,' said the girl.

Stone faced the Apache.

'Chaco, ain't it?' he asked quietly.

'That is my name,' replied the young Chiricahua brave.

'You speak English?'

'A little. Our chief, he has decreed that we braves must learn the language of the white man.'

Stone nodded. Most Indian chiefs had come to realize that the red man's day was over and that, for a red man to prosper in the white man's world, he had to be able to speak the white man's language. Consequently, they had ordered their young braves to take lessons in English. Chaco was a case in point. His English might sound a trifle stilted, yet it was grammatically correct, better indeed than either Jack Stone's or Frank McCoy's.

'You an' your band have been rampagin' all over Dawson County,' said Stone. 'Like to tell me what brought you here an' where the rest of your band are holed up?'

Chaco scowled and began to raise the Winchester, which he then pointed at the Kentuckian.

'You could lower that thar rifle,' suggested Frank mildly, 'for I don't figure there's gonna be any need for more shootin'.'

'Yes. Please do. Neither the deputy nor Mr Stone mean you any harm,' pleaded Lizzie.

'If I do, you will arrest me,' said Chaco to Stone.

Stone shook his head.

'No,' he said. 'I ain't aimin' to arrest you. You have my word.' He glanced at Frank McCoy. 'An' neither is the deppity; are you, Frank?'

The youngster hesitated. Surely Chaco deserved to be arrested for the various raids he and his band had carried out during the course of that Apache Spring? On the other hand, he realized that he and Stone would have arrived too late to save Lizzie. It was Chaco to whom she owed her life and for that he would be eternally grateful.

'I guess not,' he said quietly.

Chaco finally, slowly lowered the rifle.

'Waal?' said Stone.

'Yesterday we raided a horse ranch and released many horses. But one of our band was shot and fell from his horse. I went back to look for him while the others rode on. We are to meet up and return together to our reservation.'

'When an' where exactly are you to meet?'

147

Chaco shrugged his shoulders.

'I shall not say,' he stated firmly.

This time it was the Kentuckian who shrugged his shoulders.

'OK. Waal, go on with your story,' he drawled.

'I could not find Naches. That is the name of the brave who was shot,' explained Chaco. 'Therefore, I waited and today those men brought Naches's pony from where it was hitched in front of their ranch house and Naches from the house and they tied him across the pony's back. See.'

All three followed the Apache's pointing finger and focused on the small black pony standing a few paces behind the inert form of Little Billy Docherty. They could discern only too clearly Naches's corpse draped across the beast.

'Oh, my God!' gasped Frank.

'They brought him here,' said Chaco.

'An' you followed 'em?' said Stone.

'Yes.'

'And arrived in the nick of time,' exclaimed Lizzie. 'That one lying there' – here she pointed at the late Larry Docherty – 'was just about to shoot me when Chaco shot him.' She turned and faced a grim-visaged Sidney Bailey and said accusingly, 'You brought me here, intending to have me killed.'

She then went on to tell Stone and the deputy what Bailey had told her, that he had employed the Docherty brothers to murder all aboard the stage-coach so that nobody would suspect that the only

148

intended victim was in fact Edward Tindall.

'No, no, that ain't right. I . . . I can explain. It was like this. I had no idea that. . . .' Bailey began, but the forbidding look on the Kentuckian's face stopped him in mid-sentence.

'Put the cuffs on him, Frank,' rasped Stone.

'My pleasure,' said Frank.

'We suspected you were up to no good, Bailey, when you invited Miss Reardon on this here ride, but we couldn't figure out how you expected to git away with anythin', since your departure was witnessed by Miss Peel an' all them schoolchildren.' Stone smiled grimly and went on, ' 'Course, now it's clear as day. You was gonna claim that the Apache shot Miss Reardon an' then you shot the Apache. I 'spect Big John Docherty or one of his boys came up with that li'l scheme when they happened upon the Injun's body followin' the raid on their ranch.'

'Yeah, jest whose idea was it?' enquired Frank curiously.

'It was Big John's,' confessed Bailey, now thoroughly cowed.

Stone stepped across and peered into the gig. He immediately saw what he was looking for: a Winchester nestled on the floor beneath the seat. The conspirators had left nothing to chance. Naches had been killed by a bullet from a Winchester. Sidney Bailey had evidently planned to fire off a shot and later claim that it was that shot which had slain Naches.

149

'I guess we'd best be on our way back to town,' stated Stone.

Frank McCoy fixed the Apache with a hard stare.

'You said you was gonna meet up with the rest of your band an' head on back to your reservation. Do I have your word that you have no intention of raidin' any more ranches?' he enquired.

'You have my word,' said Chaco. 'It is my duty and my wish only to take the body of Naches back to his family. Our adventure is at an end.'

'OK. You can git goin',' said Frank.

Chaco nodded, raised his hand in a gesture of farewell and mounted his pony. He then took hold of the bridle of the pony bearing Naches's body and set off at a trot. He doubted whether he would reach Eagle Rock within the twenty-four hours he had stipulated. He strongly suspected that the remaining five young Apache braves would already be on their way back to the Chiricahua reservation. The death of Naches had meant an unhappy end to their expedition and they would all be intent on returning as quickly as possible to the bosom of their people. As their leader, Chaco had conflicting feelings; he, too, was eager to return and yet, at the same time, he dreaded the inevitable meeting with his chief. It was a sad and chastened young buck who rode eastward in the direction of the distant San Andres mountains.

Jack Stone, meantime, was organizing the others' return to Burro Creek. While Frank McCoy, still supporting a trembling and shaken Lizzie Reardon, kept his Colt Peacemaker trained on the handcuffed Sidney Bailey, the Kentuckian set about strapping the three Docherty brothers across the saddles of their horses. He used a roll of whipcord, which he extracted from one of his saddle-bags. Then he used what was left of the whipcord to string the three horses together in single file. He proposed to hold on to one end of the whipcord, which he attached to the bridle of the first horse and, so, lead all three on their journey into town.

'OK, Frank, help Miss Reardon into the gig,' he said. 'You can drive her back to town while this sonofabitch' – here he indicated Bailey with a jerk of his thumb – 'rides your hoss.'

'Sure thing,' replied the smiling deputy.

Bailey, however, was not so happy with this arrangement.

'How in tarnation d'you expect me to mount the horse when I'm handcuffed?' he protested, holding out his cuffed hands in front of him.

Stone grinned broadly.

'I'll help you,' he growled.

Without further ado the big Kentuckian grabbed hold of the hotelier and literally threw him across the back of Frank McCoy's chestnut. Then he waited until Bailey had settled himself, grabbed the reins and stuck his feet in the stirrups.

'OK,' he rasped. 'Let's git goin'.'

Straight away, they set off. The young deputy and

151

the schoolmistress led the cavalcade in Sidney Bailey's gig. Bailey followed upon Frank McCoy's horse and Jack Stone brought up the rear, trailing the Docherty brothers' three horses and their grisly burdens.

TEN

The arrival in town of the small cavalcade caused a sensation and most of the townsfolk turned out to follow it as it proceeded up Main Street towards the law office. While the others continued on their way, Frank McCoy pulled up the gig in front of Violet Peel's house, the door of which was immediately thrown open by the elderly schoolmistress.

'What on earth has happened?' she exclaimed, as she watched the cavalcade progress along Main Street.

'Miss Reardon will explain,' said Frank, as he helped Lizzie descend from the gig.

'Oh, pray do call me Lizzie!' whispered the girl.

The young man coloured, a strange mixture of confusion and pleasure suffusing his youthful features.

'May I call on you sometime, L . . . Lizzie?' he stammered.

'Yes, please,' she murmured, before hurrying up the path to the house, where she was warmly greeted

153

by Violet and hustled inside.

Frank McCoy stood for a few moments, his mind in a whirl, but a very happy whirl. Then he climbed back into the gig and headed off in the wake of the Kentuckian.

When he reached the law office he found a large crowd standing gawping at the three corpse-laden horses, and observed the town mortician, Saul Barnaby, and one of his assistants hastening across the street from the funeral parlour. Leaving them to their gruesome task, Frank dismounted and entered the office. Inside, he found Sheriff Lew Flood in earnest conversation with the Kentuckian.

'Where's Sidney Bailey?' he asked.

Flood jerked a thumb towards the door behind which were situated the law office's three cells.

'He's locked up through there an' he won't be goin' anywhere till he's brought to trial,' said the sheriff.

'For conspirin' in the murder of Ed Tindall an' the others,' drawled Stone, adding quietly, 'Bailey will hang for certain.'

' 'Deed he will,' agreed Flood.

'So, what now?' asked Frank.

'I guess all that's left for us to do is ride out to Big John Docherty's hoss ranch an' arrest the sonofabitch,' stated Flood.

'All three of us? Surely either you or me is gonna have to remain in town, Sheriff?' commented his deputy.

154

Flood smiled and shook his head.

'Nope,' he said. 'While you were gone your three colleagues returned, havin' given up their hapless search for Chaco an' his band of Apaches. Ben an' Joe have gone home while Chuck is out conductin' a circuit of the town. He'll be back here soon an' can take over while we three ride out to the Docherty place. In the meantime, you'd best fill me in 'bout everythin' that led up to you arrestin' Sidney Bailey.'

'Sure thing,' said Stone, and he and the deputy between them described the events as they had occurred from the moment of their leaving town up to the showdown at Two-Mile Hollow.

They had barely finished when Deputy Chuck Stewart, a tough, wiry-looking forty-year-old, stepped into the law office. Immediately, the sheriff briefed him on what had happened and left him in charge.

By this time Saul Barnaby and his assistant had led the three horses and their grisly burdens across the street to the funeral parlour. Most of the crowd had followed and were avidly watching the dead bodies being transferred from the backs of the horses into Barnaby's establishment.

Those remaining outside the law office fired a volley of questions at Sheriff Lew Flood when he and the others emerged from the law office.

'I'll be makin' a statement later. But, first, me an' the deppity an' Mr Stone, we got some urgent business to attend to,' replied Flood, as he and his companions mounted their horses.

Leaving behind a host of unanswered questions, they set off on the short half-mile ride to the Dochertys' horse ranch.

Big John Docherty was anxiously awaiting the return of his three sons. Although he considered his plan to have been foolproof, nevertheless he recalled that the previous plan, concocted by Sidney Bailey, had also seemed faultless. Yet, while his sons had succeeded in killing Edward Tindall as instructed, they had signally failed to eliminate all of his fellow passengers. So, he asked himself, how had they fared this time?

The appearance of Sheriff Lew Flood, Deputy Frank McCoy and the Kentuckian, Jack Stone, told him that all had not gone well. He stepped out on to the stoop and greeted his visitors, revolver in hand.

'What are you doin' on my land?' he rasped.

'We've come to arrest you, Big John,' replied Flood.

'Yeah. An' you'd best drop that gun,' added Stone in a quiet, yet ominous tone.

'An' if I don't?' growled Big John, suddenly raising the revolver and levelling it at his visitors.

Stone's reply was prompt, fast and wordless. The Frontier Model Colt was drawn, aimed and fired in one swift, seamless movement. A look of surprise illuminated Big John's rugged features as the revolver slipped from his nerveless grasp and he staggered backwards, clutching at his right shoulder. Blood trickled through his fingers, Stone's shot having passed clean through his body and buried itself in the doorpost immediately behind him.

'Holy cow, Jack! The years don't seem to have slowed you down none. That's 'bout the fastest draw I've ever witnessed!' exclaimed Flood. He turned to his deputy. 'Slap the cuffs on Big John, Frank,' he commanded.

'Sure thing, Sheriff.'

All the fight had gone out of the rancher. He meekly submitted to being handcuffed, only speaking to ask quietly that his wound be tended.

'Don't worry on that score,' said Flood. 'We don't want you bleedin' to death. Oh, no! You surely deserve a good hangin' an' we're gonna see that you git one.'

As they were busily stanching the blood and binding the wound with some bed linen torn into strips, Big John enquired, 'You gonna tell me what's happened to my boys? You arrested them, too?'

Flood shook his head.

'Nope. They're dead.'

'Oh, dear God!'

'Leastways, they've cheated the rope,' said Frank.

'Which is more'n you'll do,' remarked the Kentuckian.

Big John made no response. His head dropped and he would have collapsed had not Stone and the deputy held him up.

It was with some difficulty that they succeeded in hoisting the rancher into the saddle and then they set off on the ride back to Burro Creek.

A little later, after sending for the local physician, Doc Bates, to attend to Big John's wound, and then locking the rancher in the cell next to the one containing Sidney Bailey, the three left Deputy Stewart in charge of the law office and headed across Main Street to the Hot Spurs Saloon, where they found the mayor, Hiram C. Lancaster, propping up the bar.

' 'Afternoon, gents; let me buy you each a drink,' offered Lancaster genially.

He was drinking whiskey, but the sheriff and his two companions settled for a beer apiece.

'You got any news for me, Lew?' he asked. 'I don't s'pose you've caught either those murderin' road agents or those rampagin' young Apaches?'

'Waal, you'd be wrong, Hiram. The folks responsible for shootin' the passengers on yesterday's stage are either dead or in jail, while them Apaches are on the way back to their reservation,' replied Flood, with a grin.

'I'll be darned!' Lancaster threw back his whiskey in one long draught and declared, 'This calls for another round of drinks. An', while I'm getting' 'em in, you gotta tell me everythin'.'

'My pleasure, Hiram,' said the sheriff.

For the next hour, the events of the afternoon were related, discussed and expounded upon, and large quantities of beer and whiskey were consumed. Then the mayor and the deputy both determined to go home, while the sheriff and the Kentuckian stayed behind for one last beer.

'You aimin' on stayin' in town awhile, Jack, or d'you have to be on your way?' asked Flood, recalling that previously Stone had mentioned that he was heading south to San Antonio.

'Waal, like I said earlier, I gotta reach San Antonio in time to enlist for the cattle drive up the Western Trail to Julesburg, Nevada. Therefore, I figure on leavin' tomorrow mornin',' replied Stone.

'In that case I'm invitin' you to supper tonight, for I'd like you to meet my wife, Ellie, an' family,' stated the sheriff.

'Thanks. I'd sure appreciate that,' said Stone.

Thereupon, the two men finished their beers and, following the example of the mayor and the young deputy, left the saloon.